AN ESPECIALLY HOT SUMMER

EVERNIGHT PUBLISHING ®

www.evernightpublishing.com

AN ESPECIALLY HOT SUMMER

DEDICATION

For everyone who's had to start over—it's never too late, and you can do it.

AN ESPECIALLY HOT SUMMER

AN ESPECIALLY HOT SUMMER

Chelle de Notte

Copyright © 2019

Chapter One

June 2013

Charlie Ashton woke up to a soft paw on their arm that brought a smile to their face. "Baby." The rescue pet had come into their life too big to be a kitten anymore, too small to be a full-grown cat yet, and at exactly the right time.

Willow stepped harder on their arm, walked across their pillow, and nuzzled their face. Charlie welcomed the affection and petted her, but knew attention wasn't what she was after. "It's too early for breakfast just yet. Come on."

They dislodged Willow as they turned over. The cat jumped off the bed and onto the nightstand, where she proceeded to knock Charlie's phone to the floor with the loudest crash she could. Then she sent a tube of lip balm clattering into the wall.

They threw back the covers as she went after a

box of tissues. "All right already!" There was no going back to sleep now, and they knew from experience that it was only a matter of time before she moved on to the bedside lamp. A dent in the shade reminded them of that.

As Willow happily crunched away in the kitchen, Charlie took their pill before dealing with her litter box and the glasses, forks, and takeout containers that had piled up in the sink over the past few days. Then, after a quick shower and shampoo, they loped down three flights of stairs to pick up breakfast at the new bakery that had recently opened in the long-abandoned bodega around the corner. This place could give Lena a run for her money when it came to introducing delicious new items on the spur of the moment, which kept them coming back.

"What can I get you?" a girl at the counter with a nametag reading "Angela" asked. Her Goth makeup and facial piercings were a sharp counterpoint to her pastel apron and perky tone.

"Small coffee and a..." They paused as they looked in the case at that day's offerings. "Ooh, lemon square doughnut. That looks good."

The barista nodded in agreement. "Will that be for here or to go?"

"To go, I guess." As cute as the place was, it was also about the size of Charlie's bathroom, and the four small tables were already taken. It'd be better to eat at home.

Back upstairs, Charlie ate breakfast at their small dining table and rifled through the mail they'd been too tired to go through last night. Some new takeout menus to add to an ever-growing collection ... a thick, blue envelope that couldn't be anything but an invitation ... two belated birthday cards, and one that seemed to have gotten lost in the mail ... and an official-looking envelope with the management company's address stamped in the corner. They opened it with a curiosity that gave way to dread. Only a few lines of the long form letter sank in.

"We are writing to inform you that a deal has been signed for a condominium conversion ... expected to take 24-36 months... Current residents will have the option to buy at market rate prices... Those choosing not to buy must vacate by... If you have any questions, please contact..."

Charlie's stomach dropped further with every word. So the rumors they'd been hearing for the past few months were true, and they had no idea what the confirmation would mean for them. One of the reasons they'd moved and stayed in this neighborhood was the relatively low rent, but the appearance of the new bakery was a pretty strong indication that it wasn't going to stay that way much longer. Was there even the slightest chance they could afford to live here "at market rate"? If not, where would they go instead?

Charlie didn't have time to worry about this now, not when they had to be at work in less than an hour. They absently patted their freshly washed and styled hair into place, then headed for the subway. As they waited for the train to pull in, they sent Kelsey a text. **What's up?**

Her reply came quickly. **Hey stranger.**

Yeah, I know it's been a while. It's also been one of those days...

Say no more. My shift's over in 2 and a half hours but will you be okay until tonight?

I should be. Just getting in touch with her was smoothing the ragged edges of Charlie's psyche. They could practically hear her voice, both buoyant and no-nonsense, through the words on the screen.

Good. Same time and place.

Her next message came through immediately. **Until then, take care of yourself. Give your body the best and know you deserve it. Try that app I sent you. Be all the way in the moment.**

Thanks.

The next text came in almost as soon as Charlie sent their reply. **Call acme it. Gtg. Sry. Love ya.**

It was a mark of how long Charlie had known Kelsey that they could decipher the message that autocorrect had so badly garbled. **Be safe. Love ya too.**

The subway pulled in, and Charlie got on, trying to take Kelsey's advice to be all the way in the moment. The moment was really scary, but there was more to take note of than the news from management. The weather, for one thing—it was so warm and beautiful that they'd been able to go out without a jacket and without waiting for their hair to be totally dry this morning. Then they'd gotten a delicious breakfast and come home to their beloved pet.

And now they were heading uptown to a job they loved and one that paid well enough for them to find someplace decent, if not allowed them to stay... They forced their attention from the looming conversion, but it wasn't easy.

****

Fifty-five blocks uptown, a tall man with barely tamed dark curls was also arriving at work. The day was already getting a little warm for the suit he was wearing, but it was important to make a good impression. Besides, he got a burst of arctic air conditioning when he stepped through the revolving door.

"Who are you going to see?" a guard asked as he checked in at security.

"Bernardo Herrera."

She reached for the phone. "I'll tell him you're here."

"I mean I'm here for the company. I'm doing an internship."

"Ah. You're going to twenty-three." She handed him a pass that would take him through the turnstiles to the banks of elevators.

On the short elevator ride up, he psyched himself up as he had before every ballet. He was ready for this. He'd been through the interview process, and it had gone well enough for him to be here today. The only difference was that he hadn't spent hours rehearsing in preparation for this moment, but that was why he was here—so he could learn from the man who'd designed one of the most prestigious new performance spaces in the country.

A receptionist in casual black clothes looked at him with wide eyes. "Can I help you, sir?"

It was weird to be called *sir* by someone around his own age. "My name's Justin Robbins. I'm part of the internship program."

"Of course. Let me get Carol."

Justin waited in a chair and took a closer look around. No wonder he'd been mistaken for an executive. Most of the people bustling around the office were dressed more like the receptionist than like him. He felt like an idiot, but the importance of making a good first impression had been drilled too deeply into him.

"Justin?" A pleasant-looking woman approached the reception area. She looked around his mother's age, but he'd never seen his mother wear anything with this many artful slashes. "It's good to see you again."

He recognized the HR person from his interview and shook her outstretched hand. "You, too."

"Did you fill out the paperwork?"

"Online, and it said it went through."

She checked a tablet to confirm this. "Good. Very well-prepared." She looked askance at the couch where two guys in business outfits like his own sat with thick clipboards. "Then you can go get your picture taken for a building ID. That way you won't have to spend the summer signing in with security."

"Good."

After getting his picture taken and a few more housekeeping chores, Carol led him to the administrative team. Bernardo Herrera was the ultimate leader of the company and his department, but he'd been warned in the interview that it wasn't likely he'd see much of him. His days would mostly be spent with Conor, the project manager, and Denise, a fairly new hire who'd been in his position a few years ago.

"So where do we start?" he asked after the round of handshakes and introductions.

Denise assigned him some of the tasks she'd done in her own days as an intern. But before he could do any of them, she had to teach him the company software.

"Can I try it now?" he asked after she'd given him a demonstration on her computer.

She looked skeptical. "Of course."

Justin brought his own laptop to life, took a card from her pile, and pulled up the program. He had to ask a few questions, but managed to end with the same results she'd gotten.

She looked surprised. "Wow, you learn fast."

"Always have." It was somewhat gratifying to see that outside the studio, there was a place for his time spent watching demonstrations and then being expected to execute the same thing. At the same time, it was kind of depressing to see it play out in the office environment he'd thought he'd grow up without seeing.

At the end of the day, Justin took off his suit jacket and tie as he walked uptown with relief at moving again after being cramped up at that desk all day. It was too hot for his suit, but he should still look good enough for the restaurant. His sister had invited him to meet her there after his first day at the internship.

"Welcome to Helga's," a pretty hostess said. "Do you have a reservation?"

He didn't, but he'd heard how to get around it. "I'll wait at the bar, thanks."

"Of course, sir. Sit anywhere you want."

Justin took a seat a few stools away from a pair of women who couldn't be that far out of college and thought he'd had about enough of this *sir* business that was making him feel older than he really was. The bartender handed them a round of drinks before turning toward him.

"What can I get you?"

Justin peered closely at the server who'd addressed him. The bartender's short hair and lean stature had given the appearance of a man from the back, but the carefully made up face and high voice were starting to make him think otherwise. Either way, this person was kind of cute.

"Sir?"

The voice brought him back to attention. He didn't drink that often, but a cocktail seemed in order on the first day of his internship. "A vodka and tonic, please."

"I'll need to see some ID first."

Justin was surprised, but well able to comply. "Okay," he said as he pulled out a card and handed it over.

The bartender handed it back to him immediately. "This won't work."

Justin glanced down. He'd inadvertently handed over his student ID. "Oh, wrong one."

He put it back and handed over his driver's license. But instead of getting to work on his drink, the bartender fixed him with a stare. "So, if you were born in 1985, that would make you?"

"Twenty-eight. Or it will after my birthday later this summer." Why was he getting a math test instead of a cocktail? He knew which one he needed most at the end of the workday, and one shouldn't have been keeping him from the other.

Chapter Two

In Charlie's experience, most people were flattered when they asked to see some ID and would hand over a license with a smile. This guy hadn't been smiling at all, still had a boyish look about him, and had handed over a student ID from some college in the middle of New Jersey they'd never even heard of—for all they knew, it didn't exist. Add all that to the fact that one couldn't be too careful when it came to serving possibly underage patrons in the state of New York, and they were suspicious and ready to go the extra length.

Charlie scanned the Massachusetts driver's license under a black light they kept under the bar. All the relevant watermarks popped up under it, and there was no doubt that the picture was a reasonably close match to the man at the bar.

"Now do you believe me?" he asked.

"Yeah. Here." They handed him his license back. "Can't be too careful. We've had some problems with people bringing in fake IDs."

"But I'm not one of them." He sighed. "Look, can I talk to the manager?"

Charlie stood their ground. "I'm a managing partner. Whatever complaints you have, you can take to me."

"No complaints yet, but there will be if you don't get the manager. I wanted to see her anyway."

They wondered what this could possibly be about, but only shrugged and reached for their phone. **There's a guy at the bar who wants to talk to you.**

Janelle came downstairs a few minutes later. "How can I help—Justin? Hey!"

"Hey." His face softened into a grudging smile.

"How'd it go today?" she asked, in a tone

indicating great familiarity.

"Everything was fine until I tried to order a drink." He glanced towards them.

Charlie watched the whole thing with amazement. "You two know each other?"

He looked at Charlie with the same hostile expression as before. "She's my sister."

They reeled but tried not to show it. "So, Janelle, how old is he?"

"Twenty-seven, but he'll be twenty-eight in August."

As she spoke, Charlie silently scanned the siblings' faces. Janelle was one of the few people shorter than they, and her hair was as straight as her posture and as dark as her eyes. Meanwhile, their wavy-haired bar patron had fixed them with piercing gold and green flecks in his brown eyes, and his height was evident from the moment he'd sat down. Nevertheless, a resemblance came through as they looked more closely. The eyes were the same shape and the faces were very similar, just set in completely different coloring and body types.

"So *now* can I have that vodka and tonic?" His voice interrupted Charlie's musings.

"Of course. Coming right up." They reached for a bottle of top-shelf vodka, the better to make up for this, and prepared the drink. "Enjoy."

He nodded grudgingly and sipped the cocktail. "You can bring that with you," Janelle said. "Our table's in the back."

The two of them stepped away, but not before he'd tossed what looked like his pocket change on the bar as a tip without so much as looking at Charlie. A small crowd had gathered while all this was going on, and they welcomed the chance to step away and serve everyone else. This crowd was significantly more appreciative, but their earlier patron still rankled throughout the evening.

Hours later, when it was time to close up, they went upstairs to find that Janelle had returned to the office. "Okay, seriously, that guy's your brother?"

She sighed. "We have the same parents, but I take after Mom, and Justin's all Dad—aren't genetics fun? We're fifteen years apart, but he wasn't an accident. My parents always wanted another baby, and it just took that long before it happened again. And of course we don't have the same last name, not after he still has our parents' and I took a whole new one after my divorce. Any other questions?"

"That's all interesting, but I wasn't even going there." Heaven knew Charlie was used to delivering practiced speeches like this. "All I meant was you're so sweet and nice, and he was so … not."

Janelle sighed again. "He usually can be, but he's been having a rough time of it lately. He was a soloist with the Boston Ballet until he got hurt too badly to dance anymore. He's trying college, but has been pretty rudderless ever since."

Charlie exhaled. "Damn. When was this?"

"It happened about four years ago."

The first stirrings of sympathy started to melt away. They didn't doubt that it had been a traumatic experience, but four years was more than enough time to get better, go to counseling, and figure out what else to do with one's life. All they could do was wish Janelle a good night and head downtown.

Several subway stops later, Charlie found Kelsey waiting in front of the nondescript building on Houston Street. Her blonde hair was pulled back in a bun that still looked slick from a shower. Her top was loose-fitting in front, but clung to arms that had gotten too muscular to fit into regular clothes.

She opened those arms, and they sank gratefully into them. "Thanks for coming tonight."

She squeezed gently. "No problem. It's good to see you again."

"You, too."

"So let's go." Charlie held the door for Kelsey, and it closed as they headed upstairs.

****

After a few hours of hovering between sleeping and wakefulness, Justin gave up and turned off his alarm before it could go off. Just because he was too excited about tonight to sleep didn't mean his roommates would be happy about being woken up while it was still dark out.

As he made his way to the living area, he saw that he needn't have worried. Sergei was stretching in the living room, and Alex looked up from pouring protein powder into the blender. "Ready for tonight?" he asked.

"As I'll ever be." He played it cool, but was looking forward to playing Mercutio tonight. His promotion had been two years ago, but getting to dance the parts he'd been training for all his life hadn't gotten old yet. He'd been the first in the apartment to make the transition from corps to soloist, but had been met with hearty congratulations instead of badly concealed jealousy.

Hours later, Justin waited in the wings of the *Romeo and Juliet* production. He was in full makeup, dressed in his costume, and as warmed up as he could be. Weeks of rehearsal were drilled into his muscles, and he was all set to put them into play for the crowd that had gathered on Valentine's Day.

"*Merde*," a tall, burly stagehand whispered to him.

"Thanks." He smiled at the good wishes and the man who'd given them to him. He and Rick had been on and off for a few years before calling it off altogether, but were still on good terms.

Between his roommates' good attitude and the ability to make the transition so smoothly, he knew he'd done the right thing in coming to Boston after graduation. Leaving New York after years of ballet school there had been a little scary, but the company and everyone in it had been nothing but welcoming of the new apprentices. And now that these guys and girls had made it into the company, the near-toxic competition that had permeated his training years had faded away.

The guests at the ball parted, and he made his way onstage. This Mercutio was irresistible to all ages and genders, and he achieved that by flirting with various members of the corps as he entered the scene. He even threw a kiss to Juliet's nurse, who affected an expression of shocked pleasure, before he moved to the center for his solo. He jumped into a cabriole, then moved into a series of fouettes before his next leap.

But instead of landing on his feet to go into the next round, he was collapsed on the stage with his right leg bent at an unnatural angle under him. The corps didn't so much break character as shatter it to gape at him. The curtain flew down, but it didn't fully block out the gasps and screams coming from the audience. Not that he heard much of it over the roar of pain in his leg.

Justin woke up from a sound sleep, his heart racing just as much as on the night that threw everything into chaos. It took a few minutes to remember that he wasn't onstage, he was on the sofa bed in the second bedroom his sister used as a home office. And it wasn't fair that at a dinner where the wine had kept coming after that first cocktail, he hadn't had enough to drink to completely block out the memories, but had had enough that he wasn't sure whether his head or bladder was about to explode first.

As one humiliating experience after a frat party had been one too many, he forced himself out of bed and into the bathroom down the hall. Once all the alcohol was out of his body, he dug out the Advil from Janelle's medicine cabinet. It would work on his headache, but there wasn't a pill on the market that could help with what else was in his head. The therapists who'd come to see him after the accident had taught him to control the flashbacks, but the memory still cropped up in particularly stressful situations.

"Justin?" He heard Janelle's soft voice outside the door and opened it to see her standing there. Her hair was rumpled from sleep, and her eyes looked concerned despite being half-open. Between her expression and the age difference, it was like waking up in in his childhood bedroom. "Are you okay?"

"I'm fine. Go back to sleep."

One of them ought to, at least. He couldn't even contemplate it, but he also knew he couldn't get through a day at his internship on so little sleep and feeling so wrecked. He looked in vain for a middle ground among his clothes. In the end, he put on another suit and bought a large coffee at the cart outside the office in the hopes that it would make him look more composed and awake than he felt.

In spite of this, it was clear he wasn't fooling anyone. "You look tired," Denise said, glancing at him from her computer. "What'd you do after you left?"

"Nothing much. Those drinks must've been stronger than I thought."

Conor looked stern, and Denise assumed an expression of skepticism. "For future reference, don't bring that up at the office again. Where'd you go, anyway?"

"My sister's the manager of a restaurant, so I went to see her."

"Really? Which one?"

"Helga's."

The atmosphere in the department changed at the sound of the name. "Omigod, you're so lucky!" Denise exclaimed.

"You've been?" he asked.

"Not yet, but I'm dying to." She smiled mischievously. "Think you can give her my name to help my reservation along?"

"I took my wife for Valentine's Day this year," Conor interjected before he could answer. His face softened with a smile at the memory. "What a nice place, and that dinner was *amazing*."

"I know," Denise said. "I've seen pictures, and the menu has something else I'm dying to try every time I look at it online."

"That place could turn a grilled cheese sandwich into a gourmet meal, but that maple miso salmon..." Conor's voice trailed off. "It's going on four months ago, and I'm still thinking about it."

Justin remembered sending Janelle a congratulatory text after she'd gotten her new job earlier that spring. At the time, though, he'd been too busy trying to feign interest in his latest college program and stay off academic probation to think much else about it. Now he found himself seeing her accomplishment in a new light. Maybe he'd give the place a second chance, but no one had better question his age again.

Chapter Three

Charlie woke up feeling a little better about things the next morning. An hour or two with Kelsey usually had that effect on them, and her words of advice still rang in their ears. *"If you play as active a role in this as you can, it won't be as scary or unexpected."* Fear would appear to be a foreign emotion to a woman who ran into burning buildings for a living, but she'd managed to talk them down without making them feel condescended to. It was her gift.

That motivated them to pull the letter out and take a closer look. The last paragraph invited residents to a meeting that would cover the conversion next week, and they wrote a short RSVP email. If their home was going to be demolished, it wasn't going to happen while their back was turned. Nevertheless, the very thought bothered Charlie like a rock in their shoe.

But there was nothing to be done about it now. They fed Willow, got ready for work, put on a button-down shirt and dark jeans, and headed uptown. They were greeted by the sound of their boss singing an early contender for song of the summer. "Oh! Hi, Charlie," Lena said, stopping in mid-lyric at the sight of them.

"You're awfully happy this morning," they said by way of greeting. "What's going on?"

"Why does there have to be a reason?" Lena asked, gesturing around her. "It's a beautiful day, the sun is shining, strawberries are back in season—"

"And you're getting some. Guess I don't have to ask what you and Ryan did on your day off." Last Christmas, Lena had spent two days in bed with a six-foot-five, unbelievably jacked delivery guy from one of the restaurant's suppliers. Ever since he'd decided to move to New York, she'd been on about cloud nine thousand.

Lena shook her head dismissively, but her huge grin only proved their point. She handed them a quart of berries about the same color her face had turned. "Here. Get creative today."

Charlie popped a strawberry in their mouth as they headed to the bar. While not enough to impart Lena's glow, these were definitely delicious and would make a perfect centerpiece for summer cocktails. However, as the lunch crowd came in, they found their team pouring wine and beer more often than mixing drinks.

When they went back to the bar later that evening, their pulse spiked at the sight of a familiar face. That asshole—it was too weird to think of him as Janelle's brother—was sitting at the end of the bar. He looked better than they wanted to admit in a gray suit, a light green shirt, and a suspicious expression. "We meet again," they said coolly.

He met their eyes. "I can concede I was a bit of an ass last night, but if you hadn't wound me up like that—"

They sighed. There was nothing to be gained by the urge to spit in his drink from rehashing yesterday's incident. "I freely admit that we got off on the wrong foot, but we can get on the right one if you'll help me out."

He gave Charlie a searching look. "What do you mean?"

"My boss needs a new cocktail menu by the end of the day, but my allergies are acting up and I can't taste a thing." They affected a huge sniff. "If I make you a drink, can you do me a solid and tell me how it is?"

"What is it?"

"New recipe I came up with that sounds good on

paper, but now I can't say for sure how it's going to taste." They paused. "You don't have any food allergies, do you?"

He shook his head. "No."

"So how about this—you try this complimentary drink, give me your thoughts, and I'll give you anything you want, on me, after. Deal?"

He shrugged. "Deal."

Charlie muddled some strawberries with a few herbs in a shaker before adding a shot of vodka, a scoop of ice, and shaking up the whole concoction. They'd never had problems with allergies in their life, and of course there was no deadline—Lena had been known to add new specials to the day's menu based on what looked good at the greenmarket in the morning—but it was the best idea they had for dealing with him. Bullies didn't know what to do when met with kindnesses like this, and it made them laugh to drive jerks like that up the wall.

"Voila," they said, topping the drink with club soda, adding a halved strawberry to the rim, and handing it to him. "Now remember, you're not doing shots. Take your time, taste it, and tell me what you think."

He took a small sip. "This is good."

"Glad to hear it, but can you be more specific? What do you like about it?"

He held his next sip in his mouth a little longer. "This looks like it'd be sickly sweet, but it is definitely *not*, and I'm glad."

"Did the berry make you think that?" When he nodded, they asked, "Would you worry about that if I'd used herbs as garnish instead?"

"Probably not."

"Good. Good." They nodded as they took his thoughts into consideration and wondered if they might be able to add this to the menu for real. "Goes without saying that we could serve this at brunch, but would you order this at happy hour?"

"It would depend on what I was in the mood for, but this would definitely be in consideration." He took a longer sip, then gave Charlie a searching look as he set the glass down. "Why did you do this?"

"Because I can't taste for shit today, and because you looked like you could use a break. Janelle told me you were having a rough time of it."

Speckled brown eyes met hazel head-on. "Did she also tell you that I lost *everything* when I got hurt— my job, my home, my life? That all my ballet friends and colleagues treated me like my bad luck was contagious, and we've barely spoken since I left? That ever since I started college, I haven't been able to find anything that gets me as excited as dancing used to?"

He looked surprised by his own outburst, and Charlie was taken aback, too. They had dealt with any number of assholes in their time as a bartender, but the majority of those people had been drunk, on a power trip, or temporarily inconvenienced. This guy was truly unhappy. They kept their thoughts in check as they said, "She might have neglected to mention that."

"Well, it's all true."

They felt their expression of insouciance melt into a more sympathetic one. "Seriously, I didn't know it was as bad as all that, and I'm really sorry for you. What happened, you couldn't pay your rent after you got hurt?"

"No, I'd spent the whole time living with two other guys in an apartment that the company owned and paid for. They let me stay through my whole recovery and rehab, but once I was out of commission, I had to be out of there. I can understand that, but that didn't make it any easier." He sighed. "Everyone says I need to move on and stop feeling sorry for myself, but no one gets that it's not that easy after spending your whole life training to do something and then being told you can't do it anymore."

"Your whole life? How long were you doing ballet?"

"Since I was six. My mom works for the arts center in town, and I hung out there after school instead of going to daycare. I saw some girls jumping around in a ballet class, started trying it on my side of the glass, and the rest is history."

"Wow. I got forced into some ballet classes when I was about five, but it didn't take. I can't believe you stuck with it so well." Before he could respond or fall into despair again, Charlie extended a hand. "And I can't believe we haven't been officially introduced. Officially Charlie."

"Officially Justin." He smiled for the first time all evening and extended his hand. Their hand all but disappeared in his, but they held fast.

He looked more relaxed as he pulled away. "So, what's that a nickname for—Charles or Charlotte?"

Are you a girl or a guy? Charlie heard the question he was really angling to ask, and appreciated him at least posing it in a tactful way. "My parents named me Elspeth Charlotte Ashton after both my grandmothers."

Justin's eyes widened a touch. "No offense, but I can see why you'd go by Charlie."

"None taken. My parents tried to justify it by saying, 'it's okay to name a nineteen-eighties baby Elspeth. We can call her Elsie,' but of course every kid in my school immediately thought of Elsie the cow with that. Not to mention—well, what do you picture when you hear the names Elsie or Charlotte?"

Justin pondered the question. "Definitely someone a lot older than me. Kind of delicate and feminine."

"Well, I wouldn't say four years is 'a lot older,' but the rest was never me. Despite my mom's deepest hopes, I wasn't into stereotypically girly things growing up. Dad took pity and started calling me Charlie, and something tells me I'd still go by it even if I was cis."

"You're not? Are you trans?"

"I used to wonder if I was, but trying to dress and live like a guy full-time for a short stretch made it pretty clear that I'm not. But I *am* gender-fluid, so I can go by Charlie no matter what."

****

To Charlie's credit, Justin had completely forgotten the bad dream, tedious work projects, and everything else that had bothered him during the day between that cocktail and this conversation. He thought for a moment about what he'd just heard. "I know I've heard the term around campus, but I don't really understand it."

Instead of explaining, Charlie fired a question at him. "You don't think twice about being male, do you?"

Justin paused. "Can't say I ever have."

"Well, it's not that simple for me. Some days I'm perfectly in tune with my feminine side, some days that side feels completely alien, and some days I'm right in between male and female. It's not set in stone, so I just go with it, see how I feel, and be as flexible as possible by sticking with this look and going by Charlie and they/them instead of he or she."

He frowned. "Isn't that exhausting for you?"

Charlie's face hardened a bit. "What's more exhausting was trying to be something, someone, I'm not. Now that I'm free to express how I feel, I feel so much better."

"Sorry. I mean, not sorry things are better for you now, I'm glad ... I mean, sorry that I..." Things were so much easier in the ballet company, where his job required him to communicate through movement instead of words.

They—he locked the term in his head as firmly as he would any new choreography—relaxed at the expression on his face. "Don't sweat it. Even I didn't know there was a name for who I am until I moved to New York and someone asked me if I was gender-fluid. I mean, I went to a school that wouldn't teach evolution or anything in sex ed but abstinence, so it's not like I was going to learn about non-binary identities there."

He flinched on their behalf. "And I thought I had it rough, taking ballet lessons at a grade school where everyone else was into sports."

They winced. "That can't have been easy, either."

"Things got a little better in my teens. Once these guys saw some of my *pas* partners, found out how I spent all this time with these gorgeous girls in my arms, it's funny how the bullying died down after that."

Charlie laughed. "Like you were going to put in a good word for them after that!"

"Well, it all stopped mattering when I was fifteen. That was when I auditioned for the School of American Ballet, moved to New York, and didn't bother to keep in touch."

As a group of girls in their twenties approached the bar, Charlie smiled and stepped away to take a round of drink orders. Justin took the last sip of his drink with regret and looked down the bar at Charlie. He'd never met anyone like them, and he could say that for more than their gender identity.

Once the girls were served, they bustled back up to him. "Sorry about that. What else can I get you?"

"A water for now," he said, thinking back on his mistake from last night, "and what wine would go with the spring salad?"

"I'll have to think… We only put it on the menu a few hours ago. Did you want any meat on it? You could get it with salmon, chicken, hanger steak…"

"Steak, please."

His answer put a more decisive expression on Charlie's face. "Then definitely red. I'd say a California pinot noir would be your best bet with that."

"Sounds good."

Even so, Charlie got out a tall, stemmed glass, and poured a few drops in. They swirled the glass so vigorously Justin wondered if the wine would wind up all over his shirt, but they handed it to him without spilling a drop. "How's that? Before you answer, have some water first to get the taste of the other drink out of your mouth."

He followed their instructions, took a sip, and smiled. "Good. You really know what you're doing."

They smiled at the compliment and poured a full serving into the glass. "Thanks to years of practice and sommelier school."

"Still, you're good at this. All of this."

"Excuse me! I'd like to give you money." The call came from the other end of the bar, where a group of businessmen had taken up residence. The other bartender on duty was serving some girls in the middle.

Charlie nodded in their direction before turning back to Justin. "Gotta admire the direct approach, I guess. But seriously, I should deal with this."

"You're at work. Don't worry about it."

For the next half hour or so, Charlie was busy with bar patrons while Justin ate his dinner. The spinach, goat cheese, strawberries, and walnuts played well off each other, and the wine went as well with the meat as they'd promised. Last night had left a bad taste in his mouth and cast a pall over the meal, but now he understood why Conor was so enthusiastic and why Denise wanted to come here so badly. He took the last bite with regret and caught Charlie's eye.

"Can I get you anything else?" they asked as they approached him again.

"Just the check, please. I have an early morning tomorrow."

Charlie ran his credit card and handed him the slip. "Well, Justin, it's been a pleasure."

He smiled. "Thanks. Same."

"See you?" The greeting came out as a question.

"My internship's not that far from here. I could always stop in again sometime."

Charlie smiled. "You could. Or if you don't make it or I'm not around…" They reached for a cocktail napkin, wrote a number on it, and handed it to him before moving on. The crowd was clearly too big for one bartender to deal with alone.

Justin signed the check, left a ten-dollar bill on the bar, and left Helga's with the napkin in his pocket. It wasn't until he was on a bus from one end of New York to the other that he realized he was still smiling. He couldn't decide what his favorite part of the evening had been: the dinner or the conversation. Charlie's sparkling eyes, impish smile, and strong hands kept flickering through his head. The very thought of them widened his own smile.

Chapter Four

Despite the high school being a few blocks from their apartment, tonight's community board meeting was the first time Charlie given the place any thought. They took a seat at the end of a row filled with vaguely familiar people on the upper end of middle-aged. An official-looking group of men and women in suits was sitting up front, and a man with a wild hairdo and all-black outfit was sitting in the midst of the group.

"Thank you for coming," a woman identified as the board president said. "We have many items to get through tonight, and we'll start with Essex Café, which has submitted an application for a liquor license."

Charlie glanced at the agenda they'd gotten on the way in and saw that the board wasn't going to discuss the conversion until over halfway through the night. They let their mind wander to work, where the Fourth of July block party would be there before they knew it. While no one wanted the day to devolve into a drunken orgy, they'd still get something special from the Brooklyn Brewery and mix up a choice of cocktails. Gin, tonic, and cucumber would be refreshing on a hot day—as it would be if today was any indication—and a spiked berry lemonade would be good for those wanting a sweeter option.

The thought of the latter cocktail reminded them of the herbal strawberry drink they'd mixed last week and added to the brunch menu to great success. More specifically, who they'd mixed it for. Justin had been coming in quite a bit after his internship wound down for the day, and Charlie found themself looking forward to his visits. The color and intensity of his eyes was hard to forget, and he'd spent more and more time showing a wonderful smile. And despite everything he and Janelle had said about his injury, he still looked tall and strong to them.

"...Street will be combined into one luxury condominium as part of the new development." Finally, the only reason they were here at all. "As the buildings in question are not in a historic district, this project does not need to go before the Landmarks Preservation Commission. Nevertheless, we recognize the impact this will have on many in the community. In light of this, we would like to invite Bernardo Herrera, the man behind the Kenneth Gaffney Arts Center, the new Compuware office tower, and now this project's designer, to go into greater detail. You will all have your chance to share your thoughts and ask questions after the presentation."

Charlie would have pinned the wild-haired man as the one in charge of the project before he even stood up. "Thank you. As many of you probably know, the four rowhouses currently onsite were built in 1924. The design of the new building to rise in their place will pay homage to this period, but the interiors will have all the amenities that the modern buyer has come to expect."

He clicked his way through a PowerPoint presentation of renderings of the new building. Charlie didn't know much about architecture, but could see that this big glass box would fit in better in Midtown than anywhere around here. The same went for the interiors. This looked about twice the size of their apartment and with windows three times the size. Lena would be drooling over the kitchen, and that bathroom would be great for relaxing at the end of a long day.

The next few slides showed amenities that would be in the new building. They were used to picking up their mail from a skinny little box at the bottom of the stairs, but this new mail and package room off the trendy lobby was a whole new animal. There would also be a small gym in the basement, a lounge that could be used for working or relaxing next door, and a roof deck with views all the way to the East River. The more Charlie thought about it, the more they thought they wouldn't mind living here at all. But how were they supposed to afford it?

"Thank you, Mr. Herrera." The community board president's voice cut into their thoughts. "We would now like to open up the floor to local residents to share their opinions on the project."

The crowd erupted. "Yes, sir, I saw your hand first."

A man around Charlie's age stood up. "When I first moved to New York, no one came here unless they got lost on the way to some restaurant in Chinatown. But now I see restaurants of all cuisines opening up around here, I see people catching on to how close we are to downtown offices, and I see buyers and renters actually deciding to move down here and not feeling like they don't have a choice. It's such an exciting time for the neighborhood, and this looks like the next logical step." A few people were nodding along with him.

A gray-haired woman a few rows behind him stood up without waiting to be called on. "It's very exciting for you, but what about those of us who aren't working downtown and making enough money to move into a big fancy apartment like this? What about the integrity and history of this neighborhood? Is this going to be the beginning of the end for us, and for an area that still has character? How long before we look as soulless as Midtown?" The crowd was buzzing in angry agreement before she'd even finished.

To Charlie's surprise, Bernardo Herrera stood quietly at the podium until she was finished. "This seems as good a time as any to mention that in exchange for tax breaks with the city, the developer will set aside a good portion of units as permanently affordable housing. The city will host a lottery for these apartments, and a small percentage will be set aside for local residents."

The news didn't do much to assuage Charlie's fears. Naturally they'd be entering, but so would any number of people in this room alone, never mind all over the city. They knew better than to pin everything on this, yet didn't know what to do or where to go instead.

The meeting moved onto the next agenda item, and Charlie slipped out. Had they been watching objectively, they would have thought the whole thing had the air of a made-for-TV movie and not thought anything else of it. But since it was their building in the crossfire, they had no such luxury.

Charlie walked back to their building wondering how much longer they'd call this place home. While a stiff drink sounded perfectly warranted at a time like this, they knew better than to keep anything where they could get to it too easily. They decided to just go to bed, but sleep wouldn't come any time soon.

****

In the middle of yet another round of researching names and contact information for reporters to come to an upcoming ribbon-cutting ceremony, Justin looked up. "Is there anything else you need me to do?"

Denise looked up from the PowerPoint presentation she was working on for the Landmarks Preservation Commission next week. "I know it's tedious, but don't think of it as data entry. Think of it as getting ready for the official launch of another Bernardo Herrera building. Does that help?"

He shrugged. "I guess."

"Good. Make sure the old reporters are still there, keep an eye out for new, and now I need you to look over this presentation for spelling and other errors." Denise stood up. "And if you feel good enough about all this to do on your own, I'll see you after lunch."

She went upstairs to the cafeteria, and Justin turned back to his project. As an intern at an architecture firm, he'd hoped he'd have been allowed to do more, well, architecture work over the summer. Instead, he wondered how different this was from the tasks he might have had to do if he'd taken the Boston Ballet up on its offer.

He brought some of that up with Denise when she returned from lunch, and she looked up from her review of the work he'd finished. "I know it's frustrating, but you're not only here to learn about architecture. You're here to see life at a firm like this firsthand before you look for full-time work in the field."

When he still didn't look convinced, she added, "And you can see more of it next week. We'll need someone to take pictures at the ceremony—you in?"

"Sounds great!" Anything that got him out of this office would be, and the prospect reminded him of events he'd been to with the company.

She handed him a new project, and the prospect of the event filled him with more enthusiasm for the day's work. Before he knew it, the other interns were filing out of the office. "You can go, too," she said.

"Good night. See you tomorrow."

"No, you won't," Conor reminded him. "Mr. Herrera is giving a big presentation in the office, and we want everything to go smoothly. Because of that, all interns are being given the day off."

Justin couldn't decide whether to feel insulted at the thought of being perceived as an interruption or pleased at the thought of an unexpected day off. A nice, safe, "Oh, right" was probably the best response.

"Try not to sound so enthusiastic," he chided. "Sleep in, do something fun, and we'll see you on Thursday."

Justin headed for the elevator. Helga's was closed on Tuesdays, so he'd be home with Janelle tonight. Home for an evening of polite and stilted conversation, if that dinner at the beginning of his internship was any indication.

His phone rang, and he glanced at the screen. "Hi, Dad."

"Hi, son," Stanley Robbins's voice boomed over the line. "I'm on the train home and thought I'd check in with you. How's your internship going?"

"Not bad." It was the verbal equivalent of his shrug.

"That's all you have to say about it?"

Seeing as a connection of one of Stanley's coworkers had pointed Justin in the direction of the internship, it was probably no surprise that his dad would want to know more. Would he take Justin's ho-hum experience as a failure on the part of his connection, or a mark of his son not applying himself?

Rather than dwell on that, he struggled to think of something to say. "It's a lot of grunt work."

"That's pretty typical of any internship."

"But I get to go to a ribbon-cutting ceremony next week."

"Well, that's good!" his father crowed.

The conversation went on until Justin reached the subway and had to hang up before he lost the call altogether. On the subway, he released muscles he hadn't even realized he was tensing. Why was it so hard to talk to anyone in his family these days?

Completely unbidden, Charlie's smiling face flashed into his head. The very thought calmed him and stunned him at the same time. How had they become the easiest person in his life to talk to? It was the oldest story in the book—spilling one's workday troubles to a bartender before going home for the night—but he was hard-pressed to think of anything cliched about Charlie.

Chapter Five

As the sun started to fill their apartment with light, Charlie's ringing phone woke them up earlier than they would have liked and before even Willow would have started in on them. For one thing, it was their day off. For another, it had been a restless night after the community board meeting that had probably left them with only about five hours of actual sleep.

And the sound of the phone kept them from getting more. What the hell? They mostly communicated with Lena, Janelle, and Kelsey by text. If this was about anything less than the restaurant burning down... They picked up the phone if only to shut it up. "Hello?"

"Oh hi, Elsie!"

"Mom?" Charlie cringed at the guilt trip and the sound of the unhappy past they'd left behind in the middle of the country. They'd never been the biggest fan of their name as a kid, and they hadn't "grown into it" as their mother had predicted and hoped. If anything, they'd grown away from it with every day that passed.

They considered correcting her, but it was too early to deal with a round of recriminations followed by tears over what she perceived as their unwillingness to conform to her idea of a perfect life. After coming out, they'd agreed that she could still call them Elsie as a private nickname between the two of them, but it was getting harder and harder to take.

"Why are you calling now? Is everything okay?" Seeing as Molly Ashton was a time zone behind them, it was a valid question.

"We're fine. Dad just left for work, and I was just hoping to catch you before you went in."

They rubbed their eyes with their free hand. "Mom, it's my day off."

"Oh! I completely forgot. I'd just hoped to get in touch because it's been so long."

They tried not to sigh too loudly. "I know, and I'm sorry about that. No excuses except that work's really busy."

"I can imagine. If it's anything like that time your dad and I came for dinner, I'm sure business is booming."

"It is. Thanks." The compliment made them feel even guiltier. Her heart was in the right place, but they had no idea where her head was sometimes.

"So, what else is going on with you?" she asked.

"Well, my building's being converted to condos." Charlie hadn't meant to say anything about that, but the words had come out before they could hold themself back. Further proof that she'd called before they were totally awake.

"It is? What does that mean for you?"

"It means I'm going to have to find another place to live." The phrase crystallized their situation and scared the shit out of them.

"In New York, or would you move back home?" Molly let her voice trail off hopefully.

"It has to be New York. I'm a partner in Helga's, remember? I can't do this job anywhere else." Not to mention they couldn't move back to a place where they weren't taken seriously and whispers behind their back were the politest treatment they could expect. They'd barely left the house when they'd gone back for a few days at Christmas, but sitting under their parents' scrutiny had been unbearable.

"Right. Silly me." Molly tried to laugh lightly, but it rang hollow. "That reminds me…"

After about ten minutes of small talk and a few brief reminiscences of what former high school classmates were doing now—mostly popping out kids—Charlie hung up with a groan. They'd been in rough shape to begin with after last night's meeting, and the call, like every other when she'd used their birth name, had brought on a tension headache.

Willow lightly leaped on their chest and seemed to immediately pick up on their mood. Instead of begging for breakfast, she nuzzled their cheek, kneaded their chest, and lay down purring. The comfort of her weight and the affection she offered filled them with love and the desire to give it back several times over. Charlie hugged her, then got up to feed her and take two Advil along with their pill on the way back to the bedroom. After that, there was nothing else they could do but lie down, put on an eye mask, and think that this was one hell of a way to start a day off.

A few hours later, they woke up with Willow curled up at their side. They smiled and opened their eyes to appreciate that they felt healthier, if still restless and out of sorts. The handout had listed everything they'd need for the lottery, and Charlie dug out the folder holding their tax information so they could fill out the application. Rumor had it that even the slightest typo would disqualify a person before the rest of the application even got read, and they couldn't be too careful.

Charlie's already knotted stomach clenched as they looked a little closer: It wouldn't matter if they made a mistake because they made far too much money to think about entering the lottery. They weren't destitute enough for what the city deemed affordable housing, but not rich enough to buy an apartment in the new building. What did that leave for the middle ground? Where could they go instead?

The very thought filled them with nervous energy

to burn, so they went over the floors with a Swiffer, cleaned Willow's litter box, did the dishes, swabbed the shower, scrubbed the toilet, and made the bed with military precision. As satisfying as it was to have a clean apartment, the day still yawned ahead with nothing to fill it until they'd see Kelsey at night.

What Charlie really needed right now was an escape. They unlocked their phone and looked through the local movie times, paying special attention to the independent cinemas on Houston Street. Going to venues like this was one of the best reminders that they'd escaped to a much better place, and it was especially fun to go in the middle of what the rest of the city would call a work day.

****

A knock on his door jerked Justin out of a night that spared him the usual nightmare, but was still filled with weird anxiety dreams. "Wha…"

Janelle poked her head in. She was all dressed for work and looking at him with an expression between concern and annoyance. "What are you doing here? Shouldn't you be at your internship?"

"Big meeting, and interns got the day off."

"Oh! Sorry I woke you."

"No, I should get going anyway." He didn't want to just lie around the apartment all day. He needed to be out and about. After checking email and social media, he put on a wetsuit, layered a t-shirt and track pants over it, and headed to a public pool on the Far West Side. Swimming was low-impact enough that he could work out without putting strain on his leg, and it was a relief to be active again after days of sitting in an office. Between his sedentary internship and the delicious meals and drinks he'd been having lately, he'd have to be careful.

Especially when he considered who'd been

serving him some of those meals and drinks. Charlie knew he'd been a dancer, and he didn't want to give the appearance of a former athlete gone to seed, as some of his middle school tormentors now looked. The desire to look good fueled him through his shower, careful choice of a casual shirt and pants, and trip to the Upper East Side for lunch.

A tall man with well-toned arms greeted him at the bar. "What can I get you?"

He was the polar opposite of the person Justin had come to expect, and the sight discomfited him. "Just a water for now. Is Charlie in today?"

"It's their day off." The bartender poured his water, added a slice of lemon, and moved on to clean some glasses.

Justin sipped his water and felt the endorphins generated by his workout fade away to bereavement at the absence. He'd gotten so used to seeing Charlie's smile, chatting between orders, and seeing what was being mixed up for the night or weekend ahead. As hot as they were, he was especially taken with their openness, intuition, kindness, and sense of humor. All qualities he didn't see enough of with his sister or his coworkers.

He reached for his phone. He'd programmed the number in days ago, but hadn't had occasion to use it until today. **Hi.**

The reply came before he could close out the app. **Who's this?**

Justin. From the bar.

Oh, hey! What's up?

I have the day off from my internship and found out it was your day off too when I came for lunch.

His phone rang. "Well, damn!" Charlie's voice

rang out as clearly as if the conversation was taking place across the bar. "Only you could make me wish I was at work instead of on my day off."

He smiled at the words and the voice that had said them. "No, you've earned it. I've seen how busy things get on weeknights, and can just imagine what it's like on weekends. I just got used to seeing you around, and…"

"And I'm glad you called. We can still do something today if you want."

"Like what?"

"Like, what was the last movie you saw in theaters?"

Justin had to give this a bit of thought. "*The Dark Knight.*" His days as a dancer had kept him too busy to fit in regular trips to the movies, a habit that had obviously stayed with him after his injury.

Charlie's response was a sharp inhale. "Then I'd say it's time you updated that. Have you ever been to the Landmark Sunshine?"

"No."

"Well, it's pretty easy to get to if you're at Helga's. Just take the 6 to Bleecker Street, head east on Houston, and it's impossible to miss once you're there."

"What time's the movie?"

"I don't know yet because I don't know what I'm seeing yet. But a whole new batch of showtimes will be coming up around 3:00. Meet me at the theater and we'll pick something out."

"Okay. See you there." He took another sip of his water and felt more of a buzz than anything alcoholic he'd had here. The very thought of seeing Charlie again spiked his heart rate and brought a smile to his face.

Chapter Six

Charlie tried to create the impression of walking from one poster to another to decide on a movie, but was actually pacing to burn off excited energy. That was one of the best parts of living in New York: The whole day could change in a second, and anything could happen. They'd started the day feeling like crap, and now they were on top of the world from successfully asking—

The thought gave them pause. Whose idea was this, anyway? Justin had been the one to text first, but they'd invited him to the movies. That was one thing the condo conversion had going for it. This one big fear had seemed to cancel out all the rest and let them take chances without even thinking about it.

Charlie shook their head. There was no point quibbling over how this afternoon had come about; the important thing was that it had and that Justin was heading downtown. They were looking forward to seeing him without the bar separating them.

Speaking of which, he ought to be here any minute. Charlie glanced at the group of people heading east, and a tall, good-looking man with carefully tamed curls was among them. He was wearing dark jeans and a Boston College t-shirt, and they had to look again before they recognized Justin out of his suits.

"Hey! It's me." Charlie waved before he could walk past the theater.

Justin turned back and headed towards them with a grin. "I almost didn't recognize you."

Charlie glanced down at the dusky purple shirt they'd chosen to bring out their eyes and skin tone. "It's the shirt. I don't usually wear color to work."

"It works, but it's not just that. You seem so much taller behind the bar."

Charlie bristled. "I don't stand on a block back there, if that's what you're wondering." That dig from a drunk patron still rankled after all those years.

Justin looked surprised. "That's not what I meant. I guess you look taller back there because you rule there."

They softened a bit. "Thanks."

"I mean that in every sense of the word. Your drinks are great, but the bar's where you're in command. No wonder you stand taller back there."

Every word made them smile. "I never thought about it that way before, but you're right."

As the two of them looked up at the box office, Charlie found themself moving their shoulders back and adjusting their posture to match what had come of years of Justin's ballet training. "This one's starting in ten minutes," they said.

Justin followed their gaze and glanced at the movie's poster on the wall. "Looks interesting, but it's also in Swedish. Do you feel like reading subtitles today?"

"Uh, not really."

"How about this?" he asked, pointing to an American-made independent movie with a slightly later showtime.

Charlie looked up. "Oh yeah, that got good reviews. Works for me." They headed to the box office and bought a ticket, Justin right behind them.

"Cool place," he said upon entering the cavernous lobby.

They glanced around admiringly, too. "Yeah, it's been in the neighborhood forever. I think it used to be a vaudeville theater, now it shows movies … whatever the entertainment of the day is."

"I like it."

"Me, too. Want anything?" Charlie asked, gesturing to the concession stand.

Justin hesitated. "I don't know… Maybe just a small popcorn."

"You won't regret it," Charlie said.

His eyes widened. "Are you sure? Even that small is huge!"

"Okay, so we'll share one, please," they said, talking to him as much as the concessions guy.

They turned away from the counter, but didn't head upstairs. "What do you want on it?"

Justin glanced through the choice of flavorings with the same intrigued look Charlie had felt on their own face the first time they'd seen the selection. "We didn't have *that* at *The Dark Knight*."

"This is the only place I've been that offers them," they said.

Justin glanced at the selection and held up a shaker of Parmesan-flavored popcorn spice. "How's this?"

"Delicious." And downright odorless compared to some of the other offerings. Was he avoiding garlic or curry powder for the same reason Charlie would have? The thought perked them up even more.

Two escalators later, an usher directed Charlie and Justin to the screening room. "Almost private showing—nice!" they exclaimed, glancing around the room. There couldn't have been more than ten people in the room to see this movie in the middle of a weekday.

Shortly after everyone was seated, the lights dimmed and the previews started. The movie that followed wasn't bad at all, but it wasn't interesting enough for Charlie to forget who was sitting next to them. They kept stealing glances at Justin in the dark. Occasionally, they felt his eyes flicking towards them, too. When that happened, they did their best to stare forward at the screen and hide the smile that flickered up.

During a tense moment in the movie, they gripped the armrest. Justin had his hand on it, but he didn't move it away. Quite the opposite—he nudged his hand closer and closed it over theirs. They shifted their hand only to lace their fingers through his, and he held fast. Characters onscreen raised their voices, but they could barely hear the dialogue over the roar of their own heartbeat.

****

Justin couldn't believe what had just happened without even thinking about it. While he'd shaken Charlie's hand at the bar, this was completely different. The grip and warmth were nothing he wanted to lose any time soon, and they weren't moving, either. The plot of the movie resolved itself, but neither of them made a move to let go of each other until the lights came on and an usher came in with a broom.

"That was good," Charlie said, slowly letting go to stretch. The hand that had clutched his was dotted with fading nicks and cuts, presumably from cutting garnishes to go in their drink creations.

"Yeah, it was." He was referring to the shared touch because he couldn't remember a thing that had happened in the movie. His favorite part was when they had taken his hand.

All the moviegoers took the escalators down again, and the exit spat everyone out through a nondescript door next to the box office. The day had cooled off by a degree or two, and it would still be light for a few more hours yet.

"Nice night," Charlie said.

"Yeah, it is. Want to grab some dinner?"

"I wish I could, but I have a thing tonight. What

are you doing tomorrow?"

"I'll be back at my internship, but I was thinking of going for a drink after."

Charlie immediately picked up on his flirty tone and smiled. "So I'll see you tomorrow?"

"Count on it."

By now, the two of them had walked west and were standing outside a subway stop. The whole time, Justin had been trying to figure out what to do next. *Not* a handshake—too corporate—and he wasn't about to initiate a kiss when he wasn't sure if this was a date or not.

He decided to compromise by putting his arm around Charlie's shoulder for a half-hug. "Well, good night."

"Good night."

He was halfway down the subway steps when he heard footsteps behind him. "Aw, come back here."

He turned around to face Charlie, who pulled him into a real hug that he was all too happy to return. His arms went all the way around them, and their hold on him was surprisingly strong. Their head reached just above his heart, and the scent of peppermint shampoo filled his nose as he bent his own head.

The embrace seemed to last forever, yet the two of them separated all too soon. "Good night," he said again.

"Good night."

He all but floated uptown, and the high of the day had yet to wear off when Janelle came home from work a few hours later.

"You look happy," she said as she walked in.

"Well, it was a good day. I took in a movie, and did some laps before that."

She paused in the act of taking off her shoes.

"Should you be doing that?"

"It's one of the best exercises I could do." He paused. "And I was wondering … are there any places around here you'd recommend for a date?"

She grinned. "And when did this happen?"

"I met someone a few weeks ago." He felt weird about telling her he'd spent the afternoon with her work colleague and wanted to see them outside of work again. If the date went well, maybe he'd come clean about it.

She thought it over. "Well, there's a pretty nice bistro a few blocks away. That would be make a good impression on a first date."

Janelle still had to wind down from her day of work, but Justin had to be up early for his internship. As he lay on the pull-out sofa bed, the memory of holding Charlie calmed his thoughts. At the same time, his heart picked up and a low-level giddiness kicked in. He never knew how he'd fallen asleep, but he woke up without remembering any dreams and with a smile.

"Looks like your day off agreed with you," Denise said as he walked in.

"It was a good day. How'd the meeting go?" The date, if that's what it had been, had also fired up his work ethic, and he was ready to get going on the day's projects. Even the most tedious checks didn't seem nearly so onerous.

At the end of the day, he headed back to Helga's. Charlie was back at the bar and back in black, yet looked different somehow. Justin looked fondly down the bar until his official favorite bartender ever was in front of him with a glass of wine, a small plate of a crunchy snack, and a smile.

He looked up in surprise. "I didn't order yet."

"Well, I know you liked this wine last week. And when I saw you pick Parmesan for the popcorn yesterday, I knew you had to try these. They're fresh from the oven."

He grinned as he bit into the still-warm cheese crisp. "Thank you, for this and for yesterday. I had a really good time."

"Me, too." Charlie paused. "I'd tell you I had fun on our date, but I was never sure if we'd decided to go out on one or not."

"I wasn't either, but I am sure I want to ask you on a real date."

Charlie's warm smile stretched into a grin. "And I'm sure I want to go on a real date with you."

"So what are you doing on Saturday?"

"Working, unfortunately. But we are closed on Tuesdays."

"Okay. How's Monday night?" It was a weird time for a first date, but he wasn't opposed to it.

Charlie smiled. "Perfect, because that's not exactly the hottest time to go out for dinner. That means I should be able to get out of here by seven."

"Works for me."

Charlie got back to work, and Justin took a sip of his drink. As good as the wine was, it was also entirely superfluous. Successfully making the date had lifted his spirits better than anything even Charlie could mix up.

Chapter Seven

Justin's suggestion of a real date had been the best part of Thursday for Charlie. The pleasure of the trip to the movies, joy of the next day's conversation, and anticipation of the night had carried them through the busiest moments of the weekend and helped calm any fears about the condo conversion.

It had also given them something to think about as they lay between sleep and wakefulness. They'd wrap their arms around their chest, bask in the memory of his firm body against theirs, and look forward to holding and being held by him again. They wished they'd had the nerve to initiate a kiss at the time, and swore they wouldn't hold back on the definite date.

But now that the moment was upon them, they were too panicked to enjoy it. That evening's bartender had been stuck on the subway, which had delayed their departure and offered limited time to spruce up before rushing to the opposite side of New York as much as anyone could rush through Central Park traffic at this time of night. Charlie rubbed a subtly tinted balm into their lips and willed the taxi to move a little faster.

"Here we are." The cabbie's voice cut into their thoughts. They thrust some bills at him, all but leaped out of the car, and rushed towards the Upper West Side restaurant.

Justin waited for them under the red awning. He was still wearing the outfit he must have worn to his internship, but his tie was gone and he'd undone a button on his shirt.

"Sorry I'm late," they said. "Work was crazy."

"You're not. I only just got here myself." He held the door open and walked in behind Charlie.

A hostess who wouldn't have been out of place at

Helga's greeted the two of them. "Good evening. Table for two?"

"Yes, please," Justin said.

"Follow me, gentlemen." Charlie tried to ignore both the misgendering and Justin's incredulous look at both them and the hostess. Fortunately, heading to the table acted as enough of a distraction. They took a seat on one side of a small table slightly off the center of the room, and Justin sat across from them. A small, battery-powered votive sat in the center of the white linen tablecloth.

"Nice place," they said.

He followed their glance around the room. "Yeah, Janelle recommended it."

Before they could talk much more, a besuited waiter approached the table. "Hello, my name is James, and I'll be your server this evening. Can I start you off with something to drink?"

"Just a sparkling water for me." As tempting as a strong drink sounded at the moment, this was neither the time nor place to throw away what they'd been working so hard for.

"I'll have the same," Justin said.

The waiter left, and Justin looked at them in surprise. "And here I thought you'd know just what wine to order with dinner."

"Not until I know what you're planning to have, but I don't like to drink when I'm not working. Too much like work." No need to go into all that now.

James returned with the waters. "Are you ready to order?"

"I think so."

He hesitated before turning to Charlie and asking, "Madam?"

"I'll have the onion soup and a house salad with

dressing on the side. Both at once, please."

He wrote it down. "And for you, sir?"

Justin ordered a chicken dish before turning to Charlie. "That's all you want?"

"That should be good." While they definitely had a healthier relationship with food now than they did in their teens, they still didn't get hungry easily. And between the rush over and the atmosphere around here, their stomach was in knots. "And didn't you want wine with dinner?"

"Ah, don't worry about it. Not much fun drinking alone."

"Sorry."

"It's okay."

James had been standing there watching them through the entire exchange. "If that's everything, I'll get this to the kitchen."

"Okay. Thanks."

As he left, Justin turned to them with a frown. "What's going on?"

"Nothing, it was just a busy day. Lunch and happy hour were more crowded than I expected, we have a lot of work to do to get ready for the Fourth of July party, and tonight's bar staff was late."

His eyes widened. "That does sound crazy."

A strained silence passed before Justin spoke again. "And all that bothers you more than this? You've been called both a gentleman and madam since we got here and haven't corrected the staff once. I know I would've said something if it were me, but what should it have been?"

"Your Excellency," Charlie said facetiously, and their smile gave him permission to cough out a laugh. "Seriously, I just try not to stand on ceremony like that. I work in hospitality, so I get that this staff's probably been trained to call everyone by a title as a show of politeness, but I feel more respected if I'm treated like a regular person."

Justin looked mollified by their explanation. "Still…"

"It's not worth it. If these were people I'd have to see and work with every day, damn right I would've spoken up. But since odds are I'll never see them again, I'll let this one slide. I've found that you've got to pick your battles, and this isn't one I'd pick."

"That's still got to be annoying for you."

"It can be," they conceded, "but what's worse is being drafted into a TED Talk when I thought I was going on a date."

"Sorry."

Charlie felt themself torn between exasperation with the waitstaff and concern with how they were coming across to Justin. "It's different with you."

"How?"

"You actually ask questions instead of jumping to conclusions."

Justin's expression softened, but the waiter showed up with the orders before he could speak. Charlie stirred their soup and looked at Justin with what they hoped was a nonchalant expression. "Anyway, I know all about me and what I have to put up with, but I want to know more about you. How'd things go at your internship?"

Justin looked a little surprised at the sudden shift, but went into a story about his day and department. Charlie did their best to keep the conversation going in that direction, and it helped that his trip to a ribbon-cutting ceremony sounded pretty interesting. He asked more about how things at Helga's were going, and the swap of stories about the days started to feel more natural.

"May I clear these away?" James was back. He addressed the question to Justin's mostly empty plate and Charlie's half-full salad plate. And while a sodden hunk of bread was still in the soup bowl, they'd managed almost all the broth and some of the cheese.

He would have shown up just as they were starting to relax. "Go ahead, thanks."

Justin frowned. "Are you sure?"

"Yeah, I told you I wasn't that hungry."

As before, James watched the conversation like he was watching television. "Will there be any coffee or dessert for you … two?"

"Just the check, please." Justin spoke decisively, and Charlie nodded.

When it came, Justin reached for it. "I got this."

"Let me," they said, reaching into their back pocket for their wallet.

"Come on, I'm the one who asked."

"And are you at a paid internship?" When he didn't answer right away, they said, "Didn't think so."

Nevertheless, he held the check fast. "We'll split it, then."

"Thanks," they said, thinking they wouldn't be putting in much for a tip.

On the sidewalk, Charlie and Justin walked side by side for a little while. "I'm this way," he said, glancing west.

"And I'm getting on the subway. Guess I'll see you."

He stepped closer, and they stepped into a hug like the one they'd shared after the movie. "Well, good night."

"Good night." Charlie walked away, feeling completely unsettled. On the one hand, getting away from that restaurant let them breathe easier. On the other, they couldn't fully appreciate the release because they were too busy kicking themself for walking away so soon. It had felt too good to have Justin's body pressed into theirs again, and his spicy soap or cologne had sparked something to life in their chest and below the waist.

****

Justin saved the document, closed the program, and saw that there was still some time to kill before the afternoon's meeting. He'd done everything he could possibly think of for work and was bored stupid.

Not to mention it gave him too much time to consider that ever since Monday night's date, he hadn't heard much from Charlie aside from a cheerful text or two. Helga's had been closed yesterday, and he couldn't decide if he should go back after work today. While he'd seen flashes of their personality over dinner, they'd spent most of it almost shrunken in on themself, barely smiling or eating. Had it been the rude waiter's fault, or was it something else?

He looked at the clock again. Maybe he was done with all his work assignments, but there was still time to do something useful. He opened Google, ran a search, and looked over the short list of articles that appeared.

"I'm a guy, and my girlfriend just told me she's gender-fluid. Now what?" Not relevant to his situation— Charlie had been open with him from the start.

"What to expect from sex with a gender-fluid or non-binary partner." Seeing as he and Charlie hadn't even kissed, this one might be jumping the gun.

"10 things to know about dating a non-binary person." That might help. He clicked the link and started reading.

"Something you wanted to share with the class?"

Conor was at his side.

Justin closed out of the internet. He'd run his search in a private browser, but no filter could keep his boss from reading over his shoulder. "I'm not—I mean—"

Conor looked skeptical. "You do you outside of the office, but don't let it interfere with your work. We're going into the meeting now."

"Right." Justin gathered a pen and pad and followed his boss to the conference room with others on the team. Once Denise had arrived with a round of coffees for the principals, the meeting began. Justin took notes with half an ear while thinking about the other night and everything he'd read.

"And then there's the Lower East Side project to think about." Conor's voice cut into his thoughts.

Justin glanced up. "Really? I was just there, and that area's great."

Conor smiled. "Then you know how excited people would be to see a project like this. So many tenements are still up, and there aren't a lot of luxury condos to choose from."

Justin thought back on what he'd noticed on the way to meet Charlie. "But there's a really cool movie theater, a lot of restaurants and bars…"

"Exactly!" The meeting went by fairly quickly after that.

On the way back to work, Conor looked approvingly at Justin. "Good job on your research. That shows great initiative."

"It was more like a happy accident. I had a date in the area."

Conor smirked. "Is that why you're looking that up?"

Justin wasn't sure he liked the expression on

Conor's face, but decided not to dwell on it. Instead, he pretended not to notice and typed up a word-for-word recap of the meeting for the team. Once that was sent to everyone, he resumed the search on his phone and read under his desk as the work day wound down. There he took off his tie, undid a few buttons on his shirt, and walked to the bar at Helga's.

Charlie was back at the bar, looking as relaxed as ever as they served a middle-aged woman a bright blue drink in a martini glass garnished with berries, then turned to talk to the other bartender. Charlie smiled as they spoke, and she laughed at whatever they said.

He watched them fondly. This was the Charlie he wanted to get to know better, not the tense one who'd barely touched their food. And by what the articles he'd read had to say, he'd brought that side out in them by bringing them to that restaurant. He was sickened by the thought of causing pain, even inadvertently, to someone he'd really come to like.

Before he could dwell on it much longer, Charlie was in front of him looking pleasantly surprised. "Oh, hey! Good to see you. What can I get you?"

"Nothing just yet. I wanted to see you."

They smiled. "I'm glad you did."

He took a deep breath. "And to tell you I'm sorry."

"Sorry for what?"

"The other night. I'd hoped I was taking you someplace nice to show you I was interested, but it looked like I put you in a bad situation."

Charlie looked up and down the bar. After seeing that it was still relatively quiet, they said, "Maybe this is a better conversation for the courtyard. Mila, I'll be back in five."

They led him through a back door in the back of

the restaurant, and opened it to a small courtyard filled with unoccupied tables for two. They chose one next to a hibiscus bush, and he sat across from them.

"Had you ever been there before?" When he shook his head, they said, "Neither had I, so none of us could have known it was going to be like that."

"But once I did, I could've suggested we leave instead of still trying to wine and dine you. I shouldn't have stuck to my old dating script and made you stay at a place that was so … so…"

He wasn't sure how to finish that, but Charlie had some idea. "So obsessed with old world charm that it doesn't know how to treat clients in the new one?"

"Yeah. The place was pretty, but that staff was awful. I know what you said about picking your battles and trying not to let it get to you, but it looked like it got you too down to smile or eat. I was worried."

"Oh. That." Something in their face tightened. "I was really sick in my teens, and I swear the experience shrunk my stomach."

He frowned. "I'm sorry. What—no, you don't have to talk about it if you don't want to."

"It's okay. It was a long time ago and I'm a lot better now, but I was anorexic."

Justin swore softly. "We lost a few girls at my school to eating disorders—they didn't die. They just got kicked out of the program for health reasons," he added hastily at Charlie's distressed expression.

"That could've been me, or so I'm told. I kept it up so badly that I went down to ninety pounds, stunted my growth, and had to go on the pill to have any semblance of a cycle. I haven't even thought about falling back into old bad habits in years, but I still don't have the world's biggest appetite, especially when I'm stressed."

The whole time they were talking, Justin listened in astonishment. While the girls he'd mentioned were still alive, they'd dropped contact with everyone at school so thoroughly they might have vanished off the face of the earth. Charlie, on the other hand, had made an impression on him and everyone who came to Helga's while looking so radiant and cheerful that he wouldn't have known they'd ever had health problems. "Damn," he whispered.

"Yeah, I know I messed myself up."

"That's not what I meant. You'd already impressed me, but to overcome something like this and take such a public-facing job, and at a restaurant, no less… That's amazing, *you're* amazing, and that's why I wanted to go on a date with you. And I did the same thing I would have done with any guy or girl I wanted to win over: took them to what I thought was a nice restaurant."

The whole time he was talking, he inched a hand across the table. The admission that he'd been trying to please them, albeit in a misguided way, softened Charlie's expression, and they covered his hand with theirs. "So you meant well."

"And what's that saying about good intentions? All I thought about what worked for me then and not what would be comfortable for you now. I read some articles online, but I still have a lot to learn."

They lightly squeezed his hand. "If you want to learn by doing, let's make another date and start over."

"I'd like that, but you pick the place this time."

"Nowhere too formal." Charlie stood up looking thoughtful, then smiled. "If you really want to go to the other extreme, there's a great Chinese place near me where no one has ever been called *sir* or *madam*."

He returned the smile as he followed them back

to the bar. "I'm in."

Chapter Eight

Charlie bustled around their apartment, getting ready for the second attempt at a date and thinking about the conversation in the courtyard. While they were proud of their gender identity, they didn't choose to advertise their past health issues. But Justin had been more than accepting of all aspects of them. Not to mention that while they doubted their mom had read any of the articles they'd emailed her, he'd done research of his own volition and was willing to expand his ideas about dating. The thought made them feel more excited about tonight and better about life in general.

Charlie glanced in the bathroom mirror at the outfit they'd chosen. Neither their masculine nor feminine side felt particularly strong today, so a plain white t-shirt and jeans made a nice, classic, all-American look. Their hair looked just the way they liked it, and now they were touching up their makeup. Nothing drastic, just enough to erase any flaws and bring out their best features.

The bathroom was a little too narrow and dim to do a good job, so they moved to the bedroom with a hand mirror and the necessary supplies. Maybe that would be one good thing about moving to a new apartment: better lighting. They had a meeting with a loan officer scheduled for tomorrow, and—

The buzzer sounded to jerk them out of their thoughts. Charlie put down the eyeliner pencil, scratched Willow's ears, and headed downstairs, where Justin was waiting outside. He looked casual in a polo shirt and lightweight pants, and they smiled at the sight of him. "Hope you found the place okay."

"It wasn't easy, but I had my phone to guide me. Maybe I'm spoiled by living and working on the numbered streets."

"I'm afraid it's not going to get much easier, but it'll be worth it." The two of them took a long, winding walk west on streets that narrowed from both geography and food stands. The sidewalks were as bustling as Midtown's, albeit with a completely different crowd. The street signs and store banners started to give way from the English alphabet to Chinese characters.

"Here we are," Charlie said, stopping in front of a tiny, nondescript storefront with dingy windows.

Justin looked askance. "I know you suggested going to the other extreme, but this looks a little too far."

"Trust me on this." The door led to a small room with cheap-looking tables with no decoration but metal napkin holders. After a young hostess showed them to a table and handed them laminated menus with no greeting but a smile, Charlie took a seat facing the wall. "If you sit there, you'll get dinner and a show."

Justin's eyes widened, and they knew what he was seeing: A man with arms about the size of their waist pounding a mound of dough that got thinner with every slam. Even from here, they imagined they could hear the hiss of steam that came from the small, skinny noodles being thrown into the pot. "Unbelievable."

"Told you."

A short time later, another teenager served steaming dishes piled high with noodles and meat. Charlie had opted for pork, and Justin had ordered chicken and vegetables. They reached for a plastic fork hidden in the paper cup of napkins in the center of the table, but he had broken a pair of chopsticks apart and was easily reaching for a broccoli floret with noodles. "How are you doing that so easily?" Charlie asked.

Justin grinned at the first taste of his meal, and his look of merriment didn't fade. "The company took a few overseas trips when I was there, and this was sometimes the only silverware we got with late-night Chinese orders."

"Good for you," they said. "I've lived on Chinatown's doorstep for years and never got the hang of them. Sad, I know."

"It's not sad, but it's also not as scary as you're making it out to be." Justin reached for a second pair with his free hand, passed them across the table, and held up his other hand. "Hold them like this, and you should be able to eat pretty easily."

Charlie tried imitating his grasp, but the chopsticks clattered to the table. "See?"

"Hey, if you don't get a move right the first time, you don't walk away from the barre in defeat. You keep practicing until you nail it." He put his own utensils down, reached for Charlie's hand, and arranged the chopsticks in it. "How's that?"

They tested it. "Still kind of fiddly."

Justin leaned closer to adjust their grip, and they pressed their hand up into his. He moved their fingers around, then stroked their thumb in a way that didn't seem connected to the technique lesson. It sent a thrill through them that almost made them drop the chopsticks, but his hand kept the utensils in their grasp. "Better?" he asked.

"Yeah. Maybe I could…" They reluctantly disengaged, clasped a sliver of meat, picked it up without dropping it, and smiled as they chewed it. "Funny. It tastes better this way."

"Told you you could do it."

****

Charlie took another bite of noodles, and Justin smiled. He'd hated to move his hand from theirs, but was pleased to see them successfully navigating the chopsticks.

"So what were you doing that you were living on late-night takeout?" they asked after triumphantly grasping more noodles and meat.

"A lot of rehearsals and shows that stretched into the night."

"And other things, from what you've told me," they said. "What exactly did you say went on behind the scenes?"

Justin told stories about some of the ballet drama that choreographers never dreamed up. He expected it to be hard to talk about his former life, but it didn't hurt as much as he thought it would. Even the gonorrhea outbreak midway through junior year felt more like a sitcom's storyline than the event that ensured he was never without protection. It helped that Charlie was a good audience, gasping and laughing in all the right places and not at all shy with questions.

"And how is she still alive?" they asked after the tale of an up-and-coming ballet couple, the corps dancer the guy had slept with on the side, and a locker full of destroyed pointe shoes.

"The other girl moved to a different company, and the two of them broke up after that. They were the picture of professionalism onstage and in class, but didn't talk outside that anymore." He took a sip of his water. "But seriously, it doesn't pay to get seriously involved with anyone in the company. We all knew that hook-ups like that are stress reducers, nothing less and especially nothing more. It let us blow off steam with someone who knew exactly what we were going through."

Charlie nodded. "It can be like that at restaurants, too. This one time, an engaged couple was working together—he was a waiter, she was a hostess—but when this guy joined the staff..."

The evening all but evaporated as the two of them traded stories. Some of theirs gave him a run for his money, but he was determined to keep up. And unlike that disaster of a night uptown, every time silence descended on the table tonight, it wasn't awkward at all. It came from both of them enjoying their meals.

As he picked up some of the few noodles that remained, he noticed how full Charlie's dish still was, despite their eating with more gusto here than uptown. "They wouldn't have made you a smaller one?" he asked.

"Portion control isn't on the menu here, but it's cool. I can just get this to go and not have to think about dinner when I get back from work tomorrow night. I mean, I can't bring leftovers home from Helga's all the time."

They smiled, and he returned it. "I guess not, but I wouldn't turn them down."

By the time they left, the foreign-looking streets were still bathed in light from what had probably been an amazing sunset. Charlie had a to-go bag in one hand and Justin's in the other.

The two of them stopped in front of Charlie's building. "I'd invite you up for a nightcap, but I don't keep anything in my apartment."

"Don't worry about it. I have an early morning, and my trainers always told me alcohol would destroy everything I worked so hard for. It's a habit I've tried to stick with even after ... everything."

Charlie looked surprised. "You don't drink, but you still keep coming back to the bar?"

"Well, I try not to make a habit of it," he amended. "And the drinks are great, but I've got to say I like the company best."

"Yeah, you do meet some great people working

behind the bar." A small, pretty blush flitted across their cheeks as they smiled at him. "I won't be there tomorrow afternoon, but I'll be back as soon as I can."

"Until then..." He leaned down as he stepped closer, and Charlie tilted their head up. They wrapped their arms around each other, and he cupped a hand around the back of their head. As their lips met and they returned the kiss, all his senses perked up. The taste of Charlie's after-dinner mint was more pronounced, their hair was silken, and their skin felt smooth and warm under his fingers. The warmth and pressure of their lips sent sparks of awakening—there was no other way to put it—to his own lips, his chest, and below his stomach.

Charlie's lips were the same pale pink as a pointe shoe, and they stretched into the smile that he could never resist as he pulled away. "Good night."

"Good night."

This time, Justin didn't head back to the Upper West Side in a haze. Colors seemed more vivid, and he found that he could actually understand the subway announcements tonight. Suddenly, every show he'd ever done where a kiss woke up a princess or brought someone back to life made sense like never before.

Chapter Nine

After feeding Willow the next morning, Charlie returned to bed not to sleep, but to bask in the memory of last night. They'd lost count of the number of times they'd gone to that Chinese restaurant, not to mention the dishes they'd ordered over the years, but it had never been as good as this. There was no seasoning like good company.

They reached for their phone and pulled up the images they'd found a few days ago. All the talk about Justin's ballet career had made them curious, and they'd dug up some pictures and videos of him in his heyday. His star had been on the rise before his career-ending injury, and it was enough to think that maybe they ought to put him on their list of celebrities they'd waited on.

At the same time, they weren't just interested in the articles. His nearly naked body was lean but well-muscled, and they couldn't take their eyes off the bulge in his tights. Charlie lightly pressed their lips together to bring the kiss back to mind, thought back to his strong arms around them, and shivered as sensation wash over their entire body, as if waking it up. They turned over, slipped their hands between their thighs, and let their fingers and mind wander until a moan of pleasure escaped. Speaking of waking up, it got them too revved to lie around anymore.

Charlie got out of bed, ran a quick shower, and stepped up to the closet in a towel to try to decide what to wear to both work and the meeting at the bank. As much as they abhorred the phrase "man up," maybe that was what would make them feel more confident and get taken more seriously. With that in mind, they chose a tailored pantsuit and white button-down shirt, slicked their hair back, and faced their reflection. Sure enough, they found themself standing a little taller and more assertively.

A cup of coffee and a strawberry-filled doughnut later, they arrived at Helga's to compliments on their dapper appearance and a new shipment of wine. They rinsed their mouth out before spending part of the day tasting and making notes for Lena. The rest of it was spent helping out at the bar or in the office.

Just before 5:30, they stepped away from the bar and popped their head in the kitchen to say good-bye to Lena. "I'll see you tomorrow."

She looked up from the vegetables sautéing on the stove in front of her. "Good luck."

"Thanks. I'll need it."

Charlie's bank wasn't that far from Helga's, which meant the walk of just a few blocks wasn't enough to clear their head and calm their nerves. They tried to remind themself that the banker they were about to meet was just a person like them, trying to make it in New York, but it wasn't that easy when this person held the keys to their fate.

"Ms. Ashton?" A man in a suit approached them with an incredulous look.

"Please, Charlie's fine." Of course the banker would know the name their parents had given them, but that didn't mean they had to spend the afternoon answering to it.

"Okay, Charlie, right this way." He led them into a cubicle and offered them a seat. "So, what brings you here today?"

Charlie took a deep breath. "It's like this. I'm renting now, but my building's being converted to a condo. I really like living in that area, so I came to see about getting prequalified for a mortgage and what else I need to do in order to stay there."

"We can certainly work on that today." He asked

them some questions about their job and income, typing every answer into the computer as they spoke. Being able to tell him they were a managing partner at Helga's was good for their ego and helped them sit up a little straighter.

Finally, he paused and studied the screen. "Well, Charlie, I don't know if I need to tell you that your credit hasn't been so hot in the past."

They nodded as every good feeling faded. It wasn't something they were proud of, but they'd been living off their credit card in the months before Helga's took off and started regularly turning a profit. Before that, they had learned the hard way right after college that paying off the minimum credit card balance every month was not a financially healthy habit.

"I see that things turned around a while ago, and it's good that your debt's mostly paid off. But it'll take some time before that stain on your record becomes a blot, and that means it'll affect how much we'd be able to lend you at this point." He looked at their home address. "And because of that, it's looking very iffy as to whether you'd be able to buy in your current neighborhood or not. That area's seen a lot of growth in the past few years."

Panic gripped Charlie's stomach. "So, what does that mean? That I'll have to rent forever?"

"I can't say because I don't know. But if you do decide to buy somewhere else in the city, you've taken the correct first step by coming here."

Charlie did their best to pay attention through the rest of the meeting, let him talk them through the mortgage preapproval application, and tried not to think of going back to work and draining one of the new cases of wine. They pulled out their phone to get in touch with Kelsey and saw a text from Justin instead. **Last night**

was great.

It was impossible that they should be able to smile after that meeting, but he had that effect on them. **Yeah, the noodles were really good.**

The reply came immediately. **I wasn't talking about the food.**

Their small smile gave way to a beam, and then they remembered he couldn't see that in a text conversation. They replied with a blushing smiley face emoji.

He sent a smiling emoji before asking, **What are you doing tonight?**

My meeting's done and I'm not going back to work.

How'd it go?

They frowned at the reminder. **Not great**, they had to admit.

He replied with a frowning face, then asked, **Can I make it better for you?**

I think you're the only one who could. While a quick hook-up wouldn't solve their apartment problem, it would make things look a lot more optimistic in the very short term.

****

As usual, Justin got off the subway at 72nd Street after a day at his internship. This time, instead of going straight to the apartment, he staked out a bench outside the station. It was nice that it had been built in the middle of a small park.

A girl who couldn't have been two days out of college strolled up. "This seat taken?" she asked.

"Yeah, I'm waiting for someone." He barely noticed her, or anyone else in the crowd or coming up the stairs. Suits of all genders, teenagers, and parents with strollers the size of small cars passed through in all directions, but he still didn't see who he was looking for. Another crowd of people climbed out of the subway, and a short person in a black suit headed in his direction. Justin was all set to politely dismiss someone else, but something made him look twice. There was no mistaking Charlie's eyes and the smile that spread across their face as they got closer. He felt his own smile widening at the much anticipated yet highly unexpected sight of them.

"Looking for someone?"

He grinned up at the sound of their voice. "You. You look fantastic."

That was all he had time to say before they sat next to him, filling his nose with their scent and the space with their presence. Sitting down put them near his height, and he took advantage to easily wrap an arm around their thin shoulders. Maybe it comforted them, but it made him feel less than peaceful. Charlie leaned in closer, sending their own warmth and a wave of heat throughout his body. He turned his head to face them, and they tilted their chin to look him in the eye. The next thing he knew, they were sharing a kiss even sweeter than the first. He wound his free hand over their gelled hair to stroke the back of their neck, and they sighed and parted their lips a little further to deepen the kiss.

Just as the tip of his tongue was about to touch theirs, loud, appreciative hoots from a crowd of teenagers jolted the two of them out of the moment. Cursing those stupid kids out was the first thought that came to mind, but it wasn't enough to make him forget who was in his arms and what he wanted to do with them.

"Maybe we'd better head upstairs." Janelle wasn't supposed to be back for a few more hours, and the very thought of what could happen in that time sent a thrill through him.

Charlie grinned. "Lead on."

The two of them kept it together fairly well on the short walk west to the apartment and on the way upstairs, pleasantly nodding to the doorman and only stroking each other's palms in the elevator. But once upstairs, Justin barely locked the door behind him before enveloping Charlie again with a greater urgency than outside the building or on the street. They enthusiastically returned the kiss, and he staggered to his room.

Justin drew away reluctantly, thinking of something he'd read. "Wait, is there anything you don't—"

"I don't want you to stop." Charlie pulled him close, and he got lost in their kiss again. "Seriously, I'm open to anything. Digital, oral, penetrative … it's all worked for me."

Every possibility they listed excited Justin more. As the two of them collapsed on the unmade sofa bed, he let his tongue slide in and they enthusiastically returned it for much longer than on the bench. He hadn't pulled the shade up before he left for work, so what remained of the summer light slipped in to let him see them. He teased their jacket off their shoulders and their shirt out of their waistband. Charlie quickly unbuttoned and abandoned it to reveal nothing underneath. The sight thrilled him, as did their skillful removal of his own button-down and undershirt. He pulled them closer and let his hands wander all over their back, luxuriating in the feel of their bare chest against his.

Charlie's strokes to his back were getting lower and teasing the waistband of his work pants. Justin squeezed their ass as he kissed them harder, and they leaned into him and his growing erection. The pressure drove him crazy and sent his thoughts working overtime. It was dark enough that they shouldn't be able to see the scar… There had to be condoms around here somewhere…

Both of their hands were in his waistband now, and he felt cooler air on his thighs as his pants slid down. The second his clothes hit the floor, the phone in his pocket buzzed.

"Leave it," Charlie gasped as his hands slowed on their suit pants.

"I better check." It was lucky he did, because the alert was to a text from Janelle: **Just got off the subway and heading home. Need anything?**

"My sister's on her way home." As he spoke, his erection dissipated and the blinding haze of lust gave way to clear, pure panic and fear of getting caught in the act.

"So?"

"So this is her place." The last time he'd experienced anything like this was when a fellow corps member had been going down on him in the dressing room while a performance had taken place just feet away. At the time, the possibility of getting caught had added to the thrill of the moment and gotten him hotter. Now he wondered what his younger self had been thinking.

"*Shit!*" Charlie all but jumped off the bed to throw their clothes back on. "And if she knows about this, it's not because I told her."

"I didn't either." He wasn't the least bit ashamed of spending time with them, but he wasn't sure how his older sister would feel about him hooking up with one of her colleagues. What he was sure of what that he couldn't exactly reply to her question with **A few more hours alone so I can fuck Charlie.**

Charlie's shirt was buttoned up wrong in parts, and they haphazardly threw their jacket on over it. "I better get out of here. I'll see you later."

"Definitely."

Justin had grabbed a pair of track pants off the floor while they were dressing, and he quickly pulled a t-shirt on before giving them a quick kiss. They darted out the door, and he dropped to the floor of his room. By the time Janelle got back, he was halfway through a set of the ab exercises a ballet trainer had recommended.

"Wow, you just don't quit," she said, then took a closer look at him. "And your shirt's on inside out."

"Right. Sorry."

She went to her room to unwind, and he finished the exercises before fixing his shirt and rummaging around the kitchen for dinner. However, the heat of his time with Charlie and the terror of the last moments had killed his appetite and wired him too much for sleep to come any time soon.

When Justin woke up the next morning, it was to the realization that his longtime nightmare hadn't revisited him. Instead, he'd woken up with a throbbing erection and the rawest frustration he'd felt in months. It had been so long since he'd felt this combination of hunger, desire, and impatience that it took a few minutes to fully identify the sensation: horny as hell and desperate to act on it.

Fortunately, Janelle wasn't awake to see him in such a state. Nevertheless, he shot across the hall and into the bathroom. While he'd had a great time on that sofa bed yesterday, it wouldn't have been right to relive it there. He locked the door and dropped his sweatpants, but didn't get ready for work right away. Instead he put his hand on his cock and lost himself in the memory of how it had felt to have Charlie's body and lips pressed against his. As he imagined every delicious option they had offered, he stroked harder. The colorful memories and rich fantasies let him come in a moment of euphoria.

But despite the release his orgasm offered, it hadn't lessened his desperation to have Charlie with him again. After he took a quick, cold shower, he decided to walk to the office. If he was lucky, he'd exhaust himself and get this out of his system before he had to go to work.

Chapter Ten

"So why didn't you say you were staying there?"

About a week after their narrow escape, Charlie was sitting across from Justin at a Little Italy hole in the wall that served incredible meals. The waiter had just grated fresh Parmesan on their spaghetti Bolognese—they'd ordered a child-size portion that still looked big enough to satisfy some adults—but they were more interested in hearing what he had to say for himself beyond small talk about his workday.

If Janelle was even the slightest bit easier to hate, Charlie would have had no qualms about fucking her brother on her sofa. But once they'd found out, they hadn't even been able to entertain the idea. Her effortless running of the restaurant took quite a weight off Lena's and their minds, and she was such a sweetheart besides.

Justin slumped. "I was embarrassed."

"There's no reason to be. Lots of people in New York live with roommates." And Charlie could write a book about some of the ones they'd had over the years. "You're lucky you get to live with family, someone you actually like."

"Janelle's more like a cross between a roommate and an R.A.," he said. "Because of the age difference, she was getting ready to go away to school by the time I knew her name. Then by the time I came to New York, she was back in New Jersey. We kept on just missing each other and never getting to know each other—I got into a company so far from home, her husband got a job in another part of the country, I started college..."

Charlie listened with interest. "Then why did you two decide to live together for the summer?"

Justin suddenly looked very intent on cutting his veal chop into uniform pieces. "I had to live with someone who'd keep an eye on me if I was going to do this internship away from home. I … sort of went off the rails when I started college."

They looked at him in disbelief. No one could have become a professional ballet dancer without a lot of training and self-discipline. These days, they saw how well he was doing at his internship and how he was still in good shape. "*You*?"

He set his silverware down but didn't look all the way up. "Me. I was fine when it was just the prerequisites every freshman has to take, made the dean's list and everything, but the trouble started when I had to declare a major. First, I thought that after I got hurt, I wanted to be an orthopedist, but I was nowhere near ready for pre-med and didn't want to take all the extra classes I would've had to—otherwise I wouldn't have had my degree until I was forty."

They frowned. "If that's something you really wanted to do, it shouldn't have mattered how long it would take."

He bowed his head further and dragged his fork through a mound of steamed spinach. "Except it turned out I didn't want it. Not enough, really."

"Oh. Then good thing you dropped that program before you were too far in to turn back."

"You're the only one who saw it that way. Then I thought about being an English major because of all the storytelling I did through ballet, but that didn't really work out either. And all this time I started blowing off classes I didn't want to take, staying out late and drinking too much… No one was around to tell me no, and it wasn't pretty."

"I can imagine." Charlie would freely admit to going nuts once they'd finally put a few thousand miles between them and their parents, and they were still paying for it to this day in more ways than one.

"My parents thought the problem was me being so far from home—I was still in Boston then—but things didn't improve much when I moved back, enrolled in a community college, and lived with them. Problem is, I didn't know what to do next because I'd done too well on the core curriculum. I could do anything I wanted within my major, but I just didn't know what that was yet."

"That whole system is ridiculous, and exactly why I dropped out in junior year," Charlie said with a frown. "I didn't even know who or what I was yet, but I was expected to have the whole rest of my life planned out. How is anyone supposed to know that in their early twenties?"

Justin looked at them sharply. "I knew and was training for that by the time I was fifteen."

"Oh yeah. Sorry." Charlie stuffed a large forkful of spaghetti in their mouth to keep from saying anything else thoughtless. Their heart ached for him, and they didn't want to make it worse.

"No, *I'm* sorry." The fight seemed to go out of Justin. "At least the internship's going well enough to make me think of switching to an architecture major. Maybe that'll take better than the others."

"That's good."

"And who knows, maybe the whole thing would've been easier if I'd been able to connect with people in my classes better, but I have nothing in common with these kids."

He sighed. "These *kids*… I started freshman classes when I was twenty-four, and if I had a dollar for every time someone called me *sir* or thought I was the T.A., I'd be able to pay for my entire college experience and have some money left for grad school."

Charlie reached across the table and covered his

hand with their own. "That's not a reflection of failure on your part. The failure's these kids' for thinking you can only do things at a certain point in life and never again. They don't know what to do with someone who makes them question everything in the little life schedules they've been given since birth."

They stroked the top of his hand. "What to say to someone who's been brave enough to face down the worst thing anyone can go through and still get up and make a new life for himself."

They made their way up his arm until their hand was on his shoulder. "How to act around someone who's not going to settle for the sake of a little temporary peace, but who'll keep trying no matter how many mistakes he makes. It's intimidating, you know?"

****

The first time Justin had let all his dirty laundry spill like this, it had been with the help of one of Charlie's cocktails that might as well have had truth serum in it. But tonight, their table was the only one in the restaurant without a jug of Chianti on it. He hadn't said nearly as much to his therapists, nor to his parents or academic advisors while trying to salvage his college career.

Suddenly, he found himself wishing he hadn't brought up college. He had to go back in less than two months, and he wasn't looking forward to it one bit. Like he'd said, he was at a point where he could take all the architecture and design classes he wanted, but he already knew none of them would be as interesting as this internship where he was doing more every day. He'd miss being at a job that challenged him more than any of his professors had, and he'd miss being in such a busy and exciting city.

More than anything, he realized he'd miss

Charlie. Just the sight of their face was enough to brighten up his day, and he'd never met anyone so easy to talk to. Maybe it was their own history that made them more empathetic and receptive to confidences, or maybe it was just their warm personality that just invited him to open up. Whatever it was, he knew they wouldn't think any less of him. If anything, they'd just given his fucked-up history a more positive view than anyone else had ever presented.

Finally, he looked up and clasped their arm. "You think I'm intimidating?"

"I did because you were so intense those first times I met you. But now that I've gotten to know you better, I have no qualms about doing this." They moved their chair closer, leaned over, and kissed him.

Justin wrapped an arm around their shoulders and pulled them close. He welcomed the warmth and pressure of their lips on his again, and returned their kiss with equal enthusiasm.

After a few golden moments, the feeling of being watched nagged at him. Without turning his face away, he opened his eyes to see diners at other tables staring. Some people looked shocked; others were trying not to watch and all the more conspicuous for it, and one idiot was even shoving his phone away.

"Maybe we'd better get the check," Charlie said. They barely moved their face from his as they spoke, and he grinned at the sensation of their lips tickling his. He pressed his mouth to theirs again before reluctantly moving aside.

A smirking waiter brought the bill and a tray with two shots. "An old Italian aphrodisiac for tonight."

"I don't think we need it." The bill was split between two credit cards, and he took their hand in his free one. He opened the door for them ... and was met with a monsoon. He couldn't have said when it started raining, but the storm was now coming so thick and fast that he could hardly see the street in front of him.

"Now what?" he gasped, closing the door again.

Charlie appeared to be bracing themself. "My place isn't that far. We can hunker down until this lets up."

They opened the door, and Justin followed them out. Maybe their apartment really was a short distance from the restaurant, but trying to walk through rapidly deepening puddles with the inability to see too far ahead of him made the trip longer. It didn't help that ever since his cast had come off, his leg had dully ached when rain or snow was on the way. Every step he took sent another wave of pain rippling up.

Things improved a bit upon reaching Charlie's building, but not much. He saw their clothes dripping on the stairs as they walked up, and his own felt sodden and heavy on him. "Aren't we there yet?" he asked.

"I live in a fourth-floor walk-up." They glanced back at him. "You okay?"

"I will be once we get upstairs." He grimaced as his bad leg protested this exercise on top of the long walk to the restaurant from the subway.

Charlie looked at him more closely, and their expression softened. "Not long now."

One flight later, they were unlocking the door and wringing out their shirt. "Do you need to sit down?" they asked.

"Not yet. It'll look like I pissed your couch if I do." The walk upstairs hadn't done anything to dry his clothes.

"Crap. Hang on." Charlie disappeared into a tiny bathroom for a moment and returned with a white towel wrapped around their naked body. They handed him another one.

He couldn't help gaping at them. Their recently brushed hair still dripped, and the rain had washed away most of their makeup. Between their bare face, thin and unblemished shoulders, and the top of a chest that would make most ballerinas look busty, they looked like a teenager. "Did you take off everything?"

"Not *everything*, but there was nothing else for it. My clothes were so soaked that all I could do was hang them up to dry in the shower. Give me yours and I'll hang them up, too."

Justin stepped back and stripped, trying not to think about how out of shape he still was despite years of trying to come back. He took his shirt off without too many qualms and briskly dried his chest. Then he removed his sneakers and socks, dropped his track pants, and rapidly wound the towel as low as he could get away with around his waist. He didn't know what it said that he'd rather walk around with his cock hanging out than his scar showing, but it shouldn't show too badly this way.

He turned back around. For possibly the first time since they'd met, Charlie didn't have anything to say. The towel appeared to be slipping from their hand, but they made no move to tighten it or any movement at all. "You okay?" he asked.

"Fine. You?"

"I'll live." He hadn't gotten to be a soloist with a professional ballet company by complaining about pain.

Nevertheless, they went into the bathroom again and came back with a bottle of Advil and a glass of water. After he'd taken some, they asked, "Why don't you lie down and wait this out?"

Charlie opened the door to the bedroom and pulled back the covers on a queen-sized bed. "Wow, it's still coming down out there," they gasped. If anything, it was raining harder than before.

He nodded as he eased down and closed his eyes. The firm mattress came as a relief to his back and legs, and the bedding surrounded him with Charlie's scent. He closed his eyes to savor the good feelings that were starting to crowd out the pain.

He felt the mattress shift as they rose from it. "I'll let you rest."

He put a hand on their back. "Stay. This is nice." And it'd be nicer to have them by his side.

Charlie removed the towel, rubbed it over their head and body one more time, and lay down next to him. Tannish nipples showed the slightest hint of rigidity at the tips. He didn't know why he'd imagined Charlie would go commando, but their only clothes were a pair of simple black briefs. And despite the rainstorm they'd walked through and the air conditioner running in the next room's window, their small, compact body gave off surprising warmth.

Justin leaned closer and wrapped an arm around them. Charlie leaned in to his touch and pulled the blanket up so it covered them both. This was not how he'd imagined getting in bed with them for the first time, but he found he couldn't complain.

He found he couldn't think too much, either. Between the day's exertions, the pummeling of the rain, and the warmth of Charlie's body and the blanket, he was too tired yet pleasantly relaxed as he lay next to them. He closed his eyes to savor the moment and immediately fell asleep.

Chapter Eleven

All too soon, the relentless glare of the sun forced Charlie's eyelids open. They always closed the blinds before going to bed, so why hadn't they had the sense to last night? And why had they passed out almost completely naked? They knew they always got too cold without clothes of some kind … yet they were warm enough now.

The pressure of morning wood in their lower back woke them all the way up and reminded them of last night. The storm, which they fervently hoped the weather had gotten out of its system. Getting so soaked that they'd had no choice but to take off their clothes and shoes so they didn't drip all over the place. Justin doing the same, placing his towel intriguingly low, and showing off one hell of an upper body above it. Lying down next to him, and letting his warmth and the sound of the rain lull them into sleep at a time when they'd usually be at the bar.

He stirred next to them and smiled as he opened his eyes. "Hey." His voice was still raspy with sleep, a night's stubble had grown in, and the rain had washed all traces of product out of his hair. It looked so much wilder and softer than usual, and he looked all the more desirable for it.

"Hey." Charlie smiled back, thinking this was one of the better ways to wake up they'd had in a while.

It got even better when he wrapped his arms around them, and they pressed into him to accept a soft kiss to the back of their neck that sent a shiver down their spine. Charlie turned over and pulled him close for a real kiss, morning breath be damned, that turned into several more under the covers as his bare chest pressed into theirs.

"Is this what we would've done last night if it hadn't rained?" they asked as they took a breath.

"I hope so," he said between kisses to their throat, "and I'm glad it's what we're doing now."

"You and me—bohhh." They got cut off as his lips and teeth found a spot that sent shivers of pleasure throughout their body.

The sound of their moan seemed to encourage him. He traced a hand down their body as he kissed their lips and neck, and Charlie let their hands wander all over his back and shoulders. Whatever he did to stay in shape, it made the front and back of him feel incredible in their arms.

He paused, and his hand hovered just above their underwear. "Can I?"

"Thought you'd never ask." They took off their last shred of clothing, and took his hand to guide it. Spending the night next to him and now all this had left them wet with longing.

Justin's grin widened, and he passed a thumb over their clit. He lightly massaged it as if determined to touch every square inch, and every square inch had Charlie writhing with ecstasy on the spot. They froze as he paused, then gasped as he slid a finger inside, then another.

"Oh God. There." They felt themself clench around his fingers to keep them in place, and he showed no inclination to leave the spot now that he'd found it.

Their moan of pleasure started to rise in volume as his fingers worked harder, and he planted his mouth over theirs to block the sound. The pressure of his lips combined with the magic of his hand to send them over the edge, and he didn't pull away until they went limp, completely spent with pleasure.

They opened their eyes to see him lying back next

to them, smiling with an expression they couldn't quite place. "You look very pleased with yourself."

"It's not smugness. I liked seeing you come." His words sent another wave of euphoria through them, and they leaned into his shoulder.

They opened their eyes to see Justin sitting up in bed and glancing around the room. "Where are my clothes?"

"Hanging in the bathroom after last night, but they better be dry by now."

He didn't get out of bed right away. "My office is more casual than I expected, but I can't get away with wearing that to work."

"You work in east midtown, right?" When he nodded, they drew on memories of working around there and said, "There's a Banana Republic in Grand Central that's open early. I swear they get half their business from people who spilled coffee on their clothes on the train ride in."

"Good." He glanced down. "But I can't go anywhere like this."

Charlie's eyes followed his down to the tent that had formed under the sheets. Evidently those dance tights hadn't been lying. They carefully schooled their face against a leer, but could no sooner stop the sparkle flashing in their eye than they could control the outdoor temperature.

"If I didn't have to go to work..." His voice trailed off, and he looked frustrated.

He started to climb out of bed, but they put a hand on his back. "Let me."

Justin sat next to them, pushed the blanket down to his knees, and lowered his boxer briefs. Charlie exhaled at the sight of his carefully groomed dark hair, not to mention sizeable cock that pulsed at their touch.

He placed his hand over theirs and started to guide it, but it evidently didn't take long for them to find his preferred rhythm. He soon moved his hand away and let them completely take over. As they stroked him, they pressed into his back, lightly bit his neck, and whispered.

"Charlie." His body went rigid before he shuddered with release in their arms. After grabbing a tissue, they kissed the back of his neck, hugged him from behind, and leaned into him. The two of them stayed like that for a few more minutes until he reluctantly rose to get ready for work. They lay back down to savor the warmth and scents that still clung to the sheets.

He kissed them one more time as he left the apartment and they stood at the door in a robe. "Once we get more time…"

"I'll be counting the minutes." As he finally disengaged, Charlie had no qualms about standing in the doorway to watch his toned ass walk down the hall and head down the stairs. The sight of him and the memory of what they'd shared gave them a beaming smile, a pleasant tightness between their legs, and a sense of power that would let them take on anything.

Take on anything, they had no choice but to do now. There was way less time to bask in the afterglow than they would have liked. They still had to reluctantly wash the morning away in the shower, feed Willow, get ready for work, help get ready for the party, handle day-to-day operations, go see Lena … and Janelle.

The thought of her sobered them a bit. They'd stopped thinking of Justin as Janelle's brother somewhere along the way, but talking about her last night had forced her back to the forefront of their mind. What did she know by now, and how were they going to tell her about this?

On the subway ride uptown, part of them

wondered what business it was of hers what they did with her younger brother. They hadn't set out to start anything; it had just happened. At the same time, they knew that the longer this went on, the more awkward it would be when she finally found out. It didn't help that she handed them an iced coffee as she walked into work.

"You didn't have to do that," Charlie said.

"It was two-for-one day. No big deal," she said, taking a sip of her own.

"Well, thanks." They stirred in a bit of sugar and took a sip, all the while feeling guilty as hell.

"I figured we'd need it today with the barbecue coming up."

"I know. I can't believe it's tomorrow." Preparations for the summer event had been keeping everyone at Helga's busy. Lena would spend the day putting the finishing touches on the menu and squeezing in prep work between that day's meals. Janelle had most of the logistics in place, but there were some things that could only be attended to on the day of the event. As for Charlie, they'd mix up the large-batch cocktails first thing tomorrow morning and help her out in the office as much as they could until then.

"Me either. Think the storm bought us a good day?"

"I hope so."

She frowned. "I also hope Justin got to work okay. He didn't come home last night, and I woke up to a text saying he crashed at his date's place."

"Is that right?" Charlie concentrated very hard on the computer screen and barely kept back a sigh of relief when it started up. The better to put an end to this conversation and let them actually start working.

The next few hours passed in relative silence. Eventually, the clock on the computer caught their eye and told them the lunch rush would be starting any minute. "I'd better help out at the bar."

"Go on. Thanks for all your help up here." They headed downstairs with the oddest mix of guilt at keeping such a secret from Janelle, relief at getting away, and residual lust from the early morning.

****

Throughout the morning, the memory of his time with Charlie hung about Justin like a fine perfume. Until now, he had never seen the point of hand-jobs. But they'd taken it beyond just a hand on his cock and made it feel like a gift from one person to another rather than a quick, impersonal release. The thought that no, he couldn't have done this for himself was the last one he had before he'd come in their arms. Between that moment, spending the night with them in his arms, and their conversation at the restaurant, he couldn't remember the last time he'd felt so intimate with anyone else.

The thought of the events that preceded brought a smile to his lips and a surge of blood to his cock. The entire time he'd known Charlie, they'd done nothing but serve him drinks, let him talk, and generally take care of him. That was the first time he'd been able to take care of them, and he'd be more than happy to do it again in as many ways as he could think of.

"Justin?"

His colleague's voice cut into his thoughts. "Yeah?"

"I asked if you were finished with the gallery from Monday's site visit."

He glanced at his screen, added a few more pictures and captions, and posted it to all the firm's social media pages. "I am now. Sorry."

Denise smiled knowingly. "I guess everyone's in

vacation mode by now. If you're done with that, you can go. We're about to."

He didn't trust himself to stand right away, so he talked as he shut down his computer. "You know, if you still want to go to Helga's, you should come to the barbecue. They're hosting a Fourth of July party tomorrow afternoon."

Denise sighed with regret. "I wish I could, but I'm leaving for the Hamptons after I finish up here."

"And I'm going down the shore," Conor added. "But tell us all about it on Monday."

"Definitely." Owing to the timing of the holiday, everyone was looking at a four-day weekend and leaving early today to make the most of it. "See you then."

It was just after one in the afternoon, but the cafeteria in the office building hadn't even bothered to open for the day. It didn't matter because Justin knew exactly where he wanted to go for lunch. He undid the top button in his new shirt as he headed uptown, relishing the ability to move without pain again and anticipating the prospect of seeing Charlie.

They weren't at the bar, but a girl around his age, give or take a few years, took his order for a chicken sandwich with market-fresh tomatoes and a spicy aioli. While he waited, he sipped a sparkling water and glanced around the restaurant. A small lunch crowd had gathered, the courtyard was open, and everyone looked happy to be there.

When Charlie came downstairs, their face lit up at the sight of him. "What are you doing here?"

He felt his own lips turn up. "My office closed early for the holiday, so I thought I'd stop in."

"Then I'm glad I came down when I did. There's a lot to do upstairs to get ready for the barbecue."

"Yeah, that's all Janelle talks about."

Why was he wasting time on small talk with them? Charlie seemed to read his mind because they glanced down the bar to make sure everyone else was well occupied before leaning over to whisper, "You're driving me crazy. I see you just sitting here, and all I can think about is what we were doing this morning."

Their closer proximity and quiet voice were enough to rev him up again. "I know. I think about what you did for me, and the things I want to do with you."

"Like what?"

"Like nothing we can do in public, and nothing I feel like waiting until tonight to do. Isn't there someplace we can go?"

A smirk played across their face. "Wait for me in one of the bathrooms and we'll see what we can do."

Justin smiled, took another sip of his drink, and headed to the back of the restaurant. Sure enough, the area by the unisex bathrooms was dark and set off from the rest of Helga's. Both were unoccupied, and he closed the door to one behind him. As he waited, he let his imagination run wild at the possibilities of what lay ahead. That bowl sink wouldn't let him sit them on the counter, but maybe if they leaned against the wall exactly the right—

"Justin?" A soft knock and voice interrupted his thoughts, and he opened the door for Charlie. Their expression was casual, but their eyes fairly smoldered at the sight of him.

They locked the door behind them and all but dove into his arms, which he was happy to fling around them. Seconds later, his lips were on theirs again. It had only been a few hours since he'd left for work, yet he welcomed the kisses with the oddest and most wonderful sense of coming home after a long time away. Time seemed to vanish as his lips kept meeting theirs, and he wanted nothing more than to stay in the moment. At the same time, his cock was fairly screaming to move beyond it and rev things up.

"God, you're hard," they gasped at the pressure of his erection into their stomach.

"That's what you do to me," he whispered, letting his lips and words rumble against their ear.

Charlie shivered in his arms, but paused. "Did you hear something?"

He listened, but didn't hear anything but his own heartbeat and their heavy breaths. "Must've hit the wall."

That explanation seemed to satisfy them, because they leaned back into him and pressed their lips to his. He slid his hands down their back, teased their shirt out of their waistband, and stroked their bare skin. Charlie gasped at his touch and pressed into him. He welcomed the pressure and leaned into it, which only sweetened the torture.

His hands wandered all over their bare back, and they continued to grind into him as their hand slid into his pants and grasped his ass. To keep from finishing then and there, he tried a time-honored trick of going through the ballet positions, both feet and arms, in his head to hold back. And yet, he couldn't focus to get past second. He didn't really want to think about that because he didn't want anything to distract him from the present moment, in which Charlie was pressing against him. He slipped his hand into their pants to hold them closer and was rewarded with their gasp of pleasure.

"Excuse me! Are you okay in there?"

The knock and sound of Janelle's voice tore Justin's lips off Charlie's, but the door flew open before the two of them could do much to make this look good, or like anything other than what it was.

At the sight of her, Charlie practically sprang

from one end of the small cubicle to the other. "What are you—"

"I could ask the same of you, but it looks pretty clear," she said as she glanced from one to the other, narrowing her eyes as she took in the messy hair, rumpled clothes, and red faces with guilty expressions. "Someone had a complaint about hearing something in one of the bathrooms, but I hardly expected this."

"Oh. That." Justin's mind raced as he tried to come up with an explanation. "I wasn't feeling—I mean, I asked—"

"Save it." It shouldn't have been possible for Janelle's eyes to narrow even further, but he could barely see her pupils as her expression of shock slowly gave way to a mask of rage. "I think you both need to go home now."

Both protests tumbled out on top of each other.

"But my lunch isn't—"

"I still have to—"

"Just go."

Justin towered over his sister, and Charlie outranked her at the restaurant, but no one showed any inclination to argue with Janelle. She shook her head and walked away in disgust. Charlie turned away to readjust their clothes, and he closed the door behind him and faced the other wall so he could get himself back together. Getting caught and seeing Janelle's reaction had killed his erection, but the shock hadn't been enough to make him forget what he'd hoped he'd been getting ready to do. Now all he could do was close his eyes, breathe deeply, and wait for it to pass so he could see straight again.

"You didn't tell me anyone could walk in on us like that," he muttered as he turned back around.

"Because they're not supposed to be able to,"

they hissed as they ducked around him to flatten their hair back into place before the mirror. "I locked the door, I did everything I could think of, but management still has a key in case of a medical emergency. And if you remember, *I* asked if you heard something, *you* said no."

"Because I didn't!" he gasped as he tucked his shirt back in. "I also didn't think we were being that loud, but maybe I was wrong."

He could see his accusing expression in the mirror, and Charlie's soon matched his. "And who got me to make noise? It's not like I ran in here to touch myself."

The sexiness of the mental picture was undercut by the scowl on their face. They didn't look at him as they went upstairs to get their bag. He went back to the bar, ignoring the stares of the tiny handful of diners as he walked, to find a cooling plate of chicken at his place. He asked for his food to go, but couldn't imagine how he was going to eat it. Getting caught in the act had twisted him in knots, and Charlie's overreaction sat in his stomach like a rock.

As they walked downstairs, they passed the bar and called a quick farewell to the girl behind it without even looking at him. He quickly signed the credit slip, grabbed his bags, and rushed after them. They didn't acknowledge him until a traffic light kept them both at a crosswalk. "Sorry about that," they said, glancing in his direction.

He paused to look at them. Their posture and words were stiff, but their eyes showed some measure of softness. He wasn't sure how to respond beyond, "I'm sorry, too."

Charlie seemed to be thinking everything over. The light changed, but neither of them moved. "What do you think your sister'll do?"

"I don't know." It briefly occurred to him that he could invite them back to the apartment to pick up where things left off, but getting caught, getting into this spat, and getting the world's most forced apology had completely killed the mood. It had also driven home the fact that he didn't know his sister at all.

Chapter Twelve

Charlie smiled and handed over a cold glass garnished with slices of cucumber and lime. "Here you go, Ryan."

"Thanks." The tall, muscular man's smile widened as he took a sip of the drink. "This is quite a celebration."

As he returned to the group of guys he'd brought from his new job at the park service, Charlie looked around the barbecue. Most people left New York for the Fourth of July weekend, especially when the timing was so fortunate, and it seemed all the outliers had decided to come to Helga's. The sidewalk was so packed they could barely see the food.

With her brightly streaked hair and vivid sundress, it was easy to spot Lena in the crowd. She was making the most of her freedom to mingle among the guests after setting the entire day's prep work in motion, but her glance kept darting towards Ryan as she moved from one group to another. Whenever she spotted him, her expression softened.

Charlie understood exactly how she felt. They'd been looking around for Justin all afternoon so they could really apologize for yesterday. As a result, every dark-haired man who showed up was making their heart skip and then crash at the sight of some lesser version.

What did it say that they were still looking for him after yesterday? They knew they hadn't been an angel in the wake of being caught, but the experience had turned him into a moody monster. While they were willing to chalk the afternoon up to bad moods on both parts from being cockblocked, they still wanted to get and give a real apology, and maybe throw in a few kisses to sweeten it.

Maybe that wasn't a false alarm leaving the buffet line now. "I didn't get any food yet. I think I'll do that," Charlie said to their fellow bartender.

She smiled. "Go for it. The meat's amazing."

Charlie poured themself a glass of lemonade before joining the buffet line. Despite trying to tell the server when, they still came away with a plate overloaded with sweet and smoky-smelling grilled meat and a small tomato tartlet flaked with sea salt. And unlike the mayonnaise-laden glops from their childhood that could have doubled as the world's most disgusting ice cream, the potato salad was warm and laced with bacon.

They took it back to the courtyard where all the guests were enjoying the meals. They skirted a man trying way too hard with heavily gelled hair and bright orange pants, looked past a table of girls in their twenties who'd overdone it on the makeup—seriously, it'd be melting into their plates before the meal was over—and saw that Justin had managed to get the last free table.

They approached it, unable to decide if they were happy or annoyed to see him. "We meet again," they said, going back to one of their first conversations with him but keeping their voice cold enough to take the edge off the heat of the day.

"I wasn't sure if I should come, but I couldn't stay away." He looked up with an unreadable expression. "Want to sit down?"

They took a seat next to him because standing around with the plate and glass was getting old and keeping them from doing anything. "How was it this morning?"

"Awkward as hell." He'd opted for the savory corn cake instead of the tomato tart, and dragged it through the barbecue sauce as he spoke. "Did she give you a hard time?"

"No, but it's been too busy for us to talk." They didn't add that they'd gone out of their way to avoid Janelle, and she'd shown no inclination to talk to them. Lena, however, had been up to her ears in party preparations but still made time to tell them she didn't want the restaurant going viral for all the wrong reasons. It had been an extremely uncomfortable conversation on both sides.

"Good. I didn't want to get you in trouble." He took a breath. "I'm sorry about yesterday."

"You already said."

"And I need to say it again. I shouldn't have snapped at you like that."

Charlie felt themself soften at his words of remorse and sorrowful expression. "And I'm sorry, too. There was a right way and a wrong way to deal with it, and I picked wrong. I feel bad about it."

"Don't. It's over now."

They ate a few bites of meat that all but melted in their mouth before Justin spoke again. "And you're right, I was at fault there, but only because being with you felt so good. I just couldn't…"

They smiled for the first time since sitting with him. "Damn right you're partly responsible. What you were doing … I couldn't help moaning or whatever she heard."

He grinned and put his hand on their thigh. They put their free hand on top of his and smiled at the touch and the memory of what his hands could do. If yesterday had proved anything, it was that they didn't want his hands off them. They also couldn't wait to see what his mouth and cock could do.

Justin seemed every bit as excited, because he didn't move his hand from their leg. They kept their hand on his, too, and took their fork in their non-dominant hand. Eating the rest of their meal like this was a little unwieldy, but they'd rather drop a few bites of meat than take their hand off him. And besides, he'd seen them make a fool of themself with chopsticks—this was tame by comparison.

As Justin finished his meal and Charlie ate as much as they could of theirs, they stood up. "Come on. It's crowded. We should free up this table, and my sources in the kitchen tell me the desserts are going to be really good."

Justin followed them back to the street. "I don't have much of a sweet tooth, but do you think I could get seconds on a side? I could eat that corn thing for dessert."

"I'd agree with that," a familiar voice said. "I couldn't help sneaking a bite on the way to the bar, and *wow*."

"You made it!" Charlie beamed at the sight of Kelsey wearing a ruffled sundress and a wide smile. She was holding a heavily laden plate of food in one hand and a glass of spiked lemonade in the other, but leaned in to give them a classic cheek kiss. They eagerly returned it, leaning in for a half-hug.

They turned back to face him. "Kelsey Matthews, I'd like you to meet Justin Robbins."

"Nice to meet you." She quickly handed Charlie her drink to hold so she could shake his hand, and Justin had an odd expression on his face as she did.

"The pleasure is mine." She smiled. "So you're the reason I haven't seen much of them lately."

They turned back to him. "Justin used to be a ballet dancer, and now he's doing an internship with an architect. Kelsey's a firefighter downtown."

"Impressive." But Justin didn't say much else as Charlie and Kelsey drew close to catch up. She handed them her drink again so she could take out her phone to show off some adorable new pictures of Bandit, her rescue mutt that had become the firehouse's unofficial mascot, and they told her how things had been going at Helga's. It was good to see her again, and the conversation flowed easily.

Kelsey glanced at a group of men in FDNY t-shirts getting their plates loaded before looking back at Justin. "I'd better get back before the guys clear out the potato salad. But it was nice to meet you."

She turned to Charlie. "See you tomorrow?"

"Definitely." She was right. It had been too long since they'd made time to see each other.

Kelsey and Charlie exchanged one more hug and kiss before she headed to the courtyard with her team, and Charlie looked around. "Wow. Stranded socialites, park rangers, firefighters … we got quite a turnout this year."

"That's wonderful." Justin's smile didn't seem to meet his eyes, and he seemed to be dragging his feet back to the food area.

They paused. "You okay? Is it too hot for you?" Why was the guy wearing pants on a day like this, anyway? As fun as the barbecue was, they were counting the minutes until they could change into something cooler and more casual.

"I'm fine." He walked a few steps further with them before speaking again. "Kelsey seems nice."

"Yeah, she's great," they said happily.

"Pretty, too."

"Can't argue with that." They spoke lightly, but their stomach clenched at the idea that she'd captured Justin's interest.

A few steps later, he asked, "How'd you two meet, anyway?"

Charlie sighed. They didn't like to talk about this part of their life, but there was nothing to be gained from being cagy on the subject. Besides, if Justin could take other aspects of their history into stride, he could take this ... they hoped. "She's my sobriety partner."

****

Years of non-verbal storytelling had given Justin insights into body language, and the close interaction between Charlie and Kelsey had been that of two people who were extremely comfortable with each other, almost to the point of intimate. He couldn't imagine how else it could have gotten to that point, and certainly hadn't expected to hear this. "Your what?"

"Okay, that's not the term we use, but it's the closest I can come up with. I had—*have*—a drinking problem that seriously messed up my life, and now I'm part of a group that deals with addiction issues through cognitive behavioral therapy and other methods. She's a part of it, and we call each other when we need help staying on track."

It still didn't add up. "But I just saw you drink the lemonade."

"You saw me drink lemonade, but not the spiked stuff. Being behind the bar meant I could make myself whatever I want. See?"

They handed him their glass, and Justin took a small sip. Sure enough, it didn't have the kick he would have expected from a cocktail and continued to confuse him. "And you're in charge of the bar."

"Yeah, and a lot of people say things like, 'I'm a mixologist' or 'I'm a wine connoisseur' to hide the fact that they actually have an unhealthy relationship with alcohol. Problem is, I really am a licensed sommelier and good at mixing drinks. I've been bartending since college, learned new tricks and recipes wherever I went, and built up something of a following. That's why Lena partnered up with me to be in charge of the bar when she decided to open a restaurant in the first place."

"But if you can't drink, how can you do that?"

"By not going the whole AA route of never touching a drop again for the rest of my life. I treat drinking like a chore by having little tastes of spirits, wine, and beer to get ideas for cocktails and pairings at work, but I don't touch anything when I'm at home or out for fun."

Now that he thought about it, he realized he'd never seen Charlie order a drink when they'd been out with him. "Besides, it's not like I'm obligated to actually drink the drinks I'm working on." They paused to give him a sidelong look. "Bring it on, I've heard *all* the jokes about spitting and not swallowing."

Justin looked at them in amazement. "I wasn't going to say anything like that."

"Then what were you going to say?"

"That you called me intimidating, but you're the one who shows such unbelievable courage. The company offered me an administrative job after I got hurt, but I turned it down because I couldn't stand the thought of being around what I couldn't have anymore, day in and day out. But you face down temptation every day, mix up these amazing drinks and combinations... Every time I think you can't impress me more, you go and top yourself."

As he stroked their shoulders and looked into their hazel eyes, the heat of the day and the embarrassment of being caught yesterday faded away. All he had any awareness of was the most resilient and extraordinary person he'd ever met. He didn't know how to say any of that, so he just pulled them close. Charlie leaned into his chest, and he felt things shift back into alignment for the first time all day.

"What are you doing tonight?" he asked.

"There's no table service, so that frees everybody up to see the fireworks." They glanced up. "Do you want to go with me? Maybe stay the night after?"

Justin grinned as he heard what else they were saying. "I'd like that."

"I'll text you the address, but I'd better get back to work."

They pulled him in for a quick kiss before heading back to the bar with an undeniable spring in their step. Justin felt his own steps lighten as he got a plate of fourteen-layer cake with berry filling and a scoop of ice cream on the side. It was every bit as delicious as they'd promised, or maybe everything tasted better now that he'd sorted things out with them and had them in his arms again.

Later that night, he took the subway to meet Charlie at a park downtown. The barbecue had been too busy for him to talk to Janelle, and he'd sent her a text saying he was going to the fireworks. He'd still barely seen his sister beyond an icy encounter in the apartment that morning, and he'd be happy to wait somewhere else until she thawed out.

Charlie met him at the entrance. While the storm had dealt with the worst of the humidity, it had still been hot and a little muggy during the barbecue. They looked fresher and more casual for having the chance to change into a t-shirt and shorts since then. He'd showered and changed his shirt, but still put the linen pants back on before going out again.

"It's getting crowded already," he remarked as the two of them walked in.

"Yeah, but we still ought to be able to find something." They led him in to the park and found a spot overlooking the river. A lot of other people had had the same idea, and it was getting crowded quickly.

They stood in front of his chest to make room for others to flock in for the fireworks. "How's that?"

As he wrapped his arms around their shoulders, he welcomed their weight against him. "Perfect."

The entire show was exquisite torture for Justin. He was all too aware of their body flush against his chest and groin, not to mention the scents of peppermint shampoo, citrus soap, and something else he couldn't name but could only identify as Charlie teasing him. He was all too tempted to take advantage of the situation— everyone's eyes were on the sky, and the fireworks would drown out any gasps or moans—but Janelle's remark that anyone else would have had the two of them arrested for lewd behavior rang clearer in his head than he would have liked.

He hadn't felt such a keen sense of awareness since he was a horny teenager with a whole new appreciation for what his dance classmates could do, namely the possibilities their bodies offered. But at the time, he'd had complicated choreography to distract him, strenuous activity to exhaust him, and strict teachers to keep everyone in line. As beautiful as the fireworks were, the show offered no such distraction tonight.

"That was a good one," Charlie said, turning to face him as people started to leave.

"It was, but I've got to be honest with you." The crowd was still too loud for anyone to hear him, and he lowered his voice as an excuse to lean in closer to Charlie and put his hands on their shoulders. "I didn't really care about seeing a light show. I agreed to this because I wanted to be with you."

"Well, I'm glad. I invited you because I wanted you with me and wanted an excuse to be close to you."

They pulled their arms around his neck and leaned up to his ear. "Still do, if I'm being perfectly honest."

They nipped his earlobe, and he tightened his grip around them. "Then let's do something about it."

They gave him one last squeeze before turning with a steely look in their eyes. "My place. Now."

Chapter Thirteen

Charlie tried to lope home casually, but the thought of what they and Justin were finally about to do fired them up. They'd spent the whole fireworks show hoping he'd grind into them or slip a hand into their shorts, but he had annoyingly been the model of a gentleman. They headed south with greater urgency than the day of the storm. He had no trouble keeping up as they chose to bypass the subway—if they stopped moving for a moment, they wouldn't be able to keep their hands off him.

Once the two of them were finally upstairs, they collapsed on Charlie's bed. Willow leaped off as they landed and seemed to glare at them as she shot under the bed. They felt a pang of guilt, but forgot it and everything else as Justin's tongue traced the outline of their lips. They opened their mouth and deepened the kisses.

Instead of tearing each other's clothes off like that aborted attempt uptown, the two of them removed one piece at a time at first. He lightly stroked their bare chest, and they leaned into his touch. They removed his shirt and kissed a firm pec.

He removed their shorts and underwear in one move, then crouched between their thighs. He looked up with a question in his eyes, and they nodded. That was all he needed before lowering his head.

Charlie practically leaped off the bed at the shock of pleasure, but forced themself to hold still to enjoy his touch. They'd spent days basking in the memory of Justin's kisses, but this was a whole new sensation rushing through their entire body from the center. They reveled in the touch of his lips and tongue, and he didn't stop until their back arched as a yowl of ecstasy escaped.

He leaned back next to them, his smile tempered by a blaze of desire. They understood completely. As amazing as that had been, they still needed *him*. The glow of their orgasm still upon them, they sat up to remove his last layers of clothing.

Justin drew back as Charlie touched his fly. "Shouldn't we get the lights?"

"Why? I want to see you." An unwelcome memory intruded on the bliss of the moment. "Is it me?"

"No, you're gorgeous. It's just..." He paused. "There's a huge surgical scar on my right leg. I don't want it to freak you out."

They slowly lowered his pants and boxer briefs, squinting at his leg as they did. Sure enough, there was a long but faint white line running up his toned calf and slicing through the fine dark hair. It was visible, but nowhere near as bad as he had made it out to be.

They lowered themself to the foot of the bed, kissed the bottom of the scar, and worked their way up it with their lips and tongue before moving on to his knee and thigh. Then they took him in their mouth. He gasped, and they went a little deeper and started to move in the rhythm they remembered from their hands. He drew in a breath, so they kept it up until they felt a hand on the back of their head.

"Enough." His eyes were so dark with lust that all traces of green and gold were gone, and were fixed on them with the same intensity that had come to drive them wild. "I'm so close."

Charlie disengaged their lips and looked him in the eye. "Don't hold back. Come for me."

"Not like this. I want to be inside you when I do."

Their whole body ached with longing. "Then I'd better get you something."

Charlie reached into their nightstand, pulled out a

packet, and stood up to hand it to him. The difference between their height and his had always been obvious, but it came into especially sharp relief now. "How do you want to…"

Justin eased them back on the edge of the bed. "Lie down and raise your legs."

Charlie followed his instructions, and he stepped between their open legs, rolling on the condom as he did. "Ready?" he asked.

You have no idea, they thought, but only said, "Ready."

He held their leg with one hand and used the other to line himself up with Charlie. He teased their entrance a bit, then went all the way in. As he filled them, all they could think was, *This*. This was what had been tantalizing them all this time, and this was their reward. Lying like this let him hit areas they hadn't been able to find themself, and having their legs up sent more blood to their center to intensify every stroke.

****

For the first time, Justin didn't regret getting hurt, losing his ballet career, or wasting all that time and money in college. All of it had led him here, to this moment of finally being where he belonged: right here, between Charlie's thighs. Their skin was smooth and cool, but he could feel their body heat through the latex. He could also feel their firm grip on his cock.

"Justin." They clenched their muscles even tighter around him. He thrust with greater enthusiasm and was rewarded with the sight of their expression melting with ecstasy. He might have liked to close his eyes to fully savor the sensations, but that would have meant tearing his gaze from their face.

Satiated, they wrapped their legs around his waist and pulled him closer. He bent to embrace them, and the contact sent him over the edge, groaning their name as he came all too soon. He would have stayed chest to chest with them longer, but his legs were trembling too much for him to stand.

As he lay down next to them, Charlie looked at him with a dazed smile. "I'd always heard it was a good sign for the bedroom to be with a guy who's a good dancer."

He grinned. "I used to use that when I was out with the corps and trying to pick up girls—or guys, depending on the venue—outside the company."

"Well, I can now vouch for that." They looked at him. "What is it, your sense of rhythm?"

"That helps, but that's not all of it. As one of only two guys in the class before I left for school, I wound up learning to lift and dance with every girl—"

"Such a stud," they teased.

"Seriously, you're going to partner with a lot of people in ballet, so you learn that what might've worked with one person won't necessarily work with another." He gently kissed Charlie.

"You learn to combine your strengths with theirs, and figure out how to help each other through the choreography." He ran a hand through their artfully cut hair and stroked their back.

"You learn how to read your partner's signals." He paused to kiss their chest and sweep his tongue over each nipple, which was hardening again.

"You learn how to make them shine." He caressed their inner thigh, and they reached for his cock.

"You learn how to work together to create something beautiful." They stroked him harder, and he lightly massaged their clit in memory of how they'd reacted that morning. Between their touches and moans of pleasure, not to mention his own unwitting dirty talk, he was starting to get hard again.

Charlie pressed into him. "And I will be happy to rehearse with you any time you want."

"Rehearse?"

"You started this metaphor, not me."

They turned over and spooned against his side. He quickly reached for another condom, then turned over and easily slid into them from behind. They enthusiastically leaned into him, and the two of them continued to learn how to move together.

Chapter Fourteen

Charlie woke up grinning the next morning. Sometimes anticipation was sweeter than the event itself, but they were pleased to know that that had *not* been the case with Justin. The sight of his bare back and mussed hair reminded them of what they'd been doing that had knocked them both out for the night.

"Your alarm," he muttered into his pillow.

They reached for their phone only to see that they hadn't set it. Willow, however, was sitting on the nightstand and chirping. As winsome as she looked, she was also fixing them with an expression that suggested she'd claw their eyes out if she didn't get what she wanted.

"Hang on." They reluctantly climbed out of bed, put Justin's t-shirt on, fed their cat in the kitchen, and closed the door firmly behind them. "I love her, but I didn't want her pouncing on anyone or nipping anybody's ankles while…"

Justin was now sitting up in bed with the sheets pooled around his waist. He'd been a little groggy when Willow had woken them up, but looked thoroughly awake and sexy now. "While what?"

The shirt was practically knee-length on them, and they pulled it over their head as they walked toward the bed. "I have to go to work, but I do have some time before that."

He pulled them close, and they wrapped both arms around his shoulders. Last night had thoroughly obliterated all hints of trepidation, and their hands wandered over each other's bodies with greater confidence. The next thing they knew, he was moving on top of them as they pulled his firm chest close to their own, thoroughly enjoying every part that touched him.

By the time the two of them finally got dressed and left the apartment, Charlie's feet barely touched the ground. Whatever reason Justin wanted to give for his prowess, they couldn't remember the last time they'd gotten out of bed feeling this good. Every time they snuck a glance at him, he didn't even try to hide his smile.

To make the most of their time with him, they walked a little further out of their way to the 6 train. The two of them bought iced coffees at a stand about the size of Charlie's bathroom and sipped the drinks on the walk northwest. Living this far from the most direct route to work usually irked them, but they embraced it today for allowing more time together.

"That's me," Charlie said as they reached the subway stop.

Justin threw out his empty cup before wrapping his arms around them. Being downtown with him like this reminded them of after the movie "date", but they kissed him this time. "I'll text you later," he said.

"Definitely. I have the thing tonight, but I'll be around this weekend."

"Great." One more kiss, and they spent the ride uptown in a happy haze. It was lucky they'd walked to take a direct train, as otherwise they might have missed the connection and wound up on the Upper West Side before they could turn around.

Their good mood dented upon arriving at work and seeing a stiff-looking Janelle walking in ahead of them. Yesterday's event had been so busy that they'd barely had the chance to exchange more than two words with her. Today, however, the restaurant was significantly quieter.

"Morning," she said coldly as she held the door open.

"Hey," they answered, nodding in thanks.

"I'm glad the barbecue went well."

"Yeah, everybody had a good time."

"And we took in a lot of money."

If they danced around the subject anymore, Charlie could audition to take Justin's place in the ballet company. "Let's just come out and say that the other day was awkward as hell."

Janelle sighed. "You're both consenting adults, and there's nothing I can say or do about it. I'm just worried."

"Why do you say that?"

"Because ever since Justin got hurt and had to make a new plan for his life, he's been completely adrift and having such a rough time. I don't want to see anyone get hurt."

Charlie was stung. "Give us both a little credit! First off, I know you told me about the big age difference between you two the day I met him, but you also told me that he's almost twenty-eight. He left home before he was old enough to go for a learner's permit, he got near the top of his chosen field, and he's lived on his own for about half his life. Does that sound like your little brother's still a baby to you?"

Janelle looked flustered. "Well, no, but—"

"But what? You're selling him short and telling me that you don't trust me to know how to be with anyone."

"And I'm also thinking of you," she said heatedly, as if in determination to get the last word. "I don't know if he told you, but he wasn't exactly a paragon of monogamy with his ballet boyfriends and girlfriends."

"He did, and what does that mean? That I should define him by the past and not give him a chance in the present? I wouldn't be working here if Lena had done that, and that's not the point. The point is that more we've gotten to know each other, the more we've come to admire and care about each other. And that tells me I'd never do anything to hurt him, and he wouldn't do anything to hurt me."

The more Charlie spoke, the more they realized it was true. Of all the people they'd ever been with, none had been nearly as interesting, determined, or sensitive to their needs and desires as Justin. True, the courtship had gotten off to a rocky start, but they and he had both been able to sort things out instead of giving up. And all the interruptions and time constraints had turned out to be good things that let the two of them get to know each other's bodies and made sex better.

"Hey, what's going on?" Lena asked, poking her head out of the kitchen at the sound of the raised voices.

Janelle looked away. "Nothing."

Lena didn't look convinced and glanced at them. "Charlie?"

"Nothing. Bit of a misunderstanding, but it's all cleared up now." Indeed, things were much clearer than they had ever expected.

****

As Justin headed west, he couldn't keep the smile off his face. While he'd spent nights in similar ways over the past few years, he'd tended to wake up with a pounding headache and wariness of what, if anything, was going to happen next with his then-partner. He didn't know what was going to happen next with Charlie either, but would welcome whatever came with open arms.

The closer he got to Soho, the more crowded the streets became. He couldn't believe it was this packed on a Friday morning, but it was abundantly clear that he wasn't the only one who'd been given the day off for the Fourth of July and hadn't gone away for the weekend. Whether because of the growing crowd or the climbing sun, it was getting hotter the more he walked. His pants were linen, but the fabric felt like the heaviest wool on his legs.

It also felt utterly ridiculous after last night. After one too many people had been freaked out by the angry red scar on his leg soon after the surgery, he'd thought it best to live in pants and have sex exclusively with the lights off. The mindset had clearly stuck with him after years had passed to allow the scar to fade.

He'd warned Charlie about it, but they hadn't cared at all. If anything, they'd used it as a map guiding their way up to his cock. The very memory sent a shiver through his body, but the suffocation of the fabric on his leg tempered the thrill.

Enough was enough. He ducked into a two-level Uniqlo and took the stairs to the men's section. The arctic air conditioning was welcome, but he'd leave feeling better if he found what he wanted. It had been so long since he'd worn shorts that he initially wasn't sure how he was supposed to look in them, but a friendly salesman assured him he was fine. The fact that he didn't flinch at the sight of Justin's bare calf either helped, too.

"Can I change before I go out again?" he asked as he paid for two pairs.

The cashier glanced down at the pants he was wearing. "Of course."

"Thanks." Justin ducked into a fitting room, moved his wallet and phone to the dark gray pair, and stuffed the pants in the bag once he was dressed again. He checked on the scar in the mirror, but wasn't bothered enough by it to cover it up again. New York summers were too hot for such self-consciousness.

He left the store feeling lighter and more relieved, and without the stares he'd come to expect from going out in shorts. How long had the surgical scar truly been conspicuous, and how long had it all been in his head? He had no way of knowing, but he did know he had Charlie to thank for getting him past that. Now he was ready for—

The thought stopped him. What *was* he going to do with the rest of the day? Nearly every minute of his days had been accounted for when he'd been in ballet school and the company, and even his worst days of college had provided some semblance of structure. He couldn't remember the last time he'd had this kind of freedom and wasn't entirely used to it. Nevertheless, he smiled at the idea.

As he waited to cross the street, his phone buzzed in his pocket. His heart spiked a little. Was it them?

He was ashamed to feel crestfallen when he pulled out his phone and saw an incoming call from Janelle. "Hello?"

"Hi," his sister said in a smaller voice than he was used to hearing from her. "Where are you?"

"Downtown. I'm off for the holiday." He wasn't sure how much to elaborate on this. "Aren't you at work?"

"Yeah, but I was wondering … are you doing anything tonight?"

"I don't think so. Why?"

She didn't answer right away. "Can we have dinner, just the two of us?"

"Okay." He drew out the word as he tried to figure out what his sister was up to. "Should I meet you at work?"

"No, I want to go home, change, and go someplace local."

He hesitated. "As long as it's not that bistro you suggested. The waiters were idiots."

"No, that's way too fancy for a weekday. I'll figure something out. How about we meet at home at seven and leave together?"

"That could work."

"Great. See you then." She hung up before he could say anything else, leaving him to wonder about what had brought this on and what lay ahead.

Chapter Fifteen

After a much quieter Friday evening at the restaurant than they were used to, Charlie met Kelsey at their usual downtown spot. She hadn't been on shift and looked more casual for it.

"So how's it going with what's-his-name?" she asked as they headed upstairs.

"Justin? What about him?" They struggled to maintain a poker face, but felt their lips twitching up just at saying his name.

"I saw the way you two were looking at each other at the barbecue, and I totally get it."

The smile was too big to contain anymore. "Good. I mean, things are good with him. Great, now that I think about it."

She smiled back. "I'm glad, but I don't know if it's exactly meeting conversation. Want to get dinner after?"

"Let's see how it goes tonight, but I like that idea." Now that the air was clear with Janelle, they wanted to tell the world about him.

By now, they were in the small office used for meetings. Only about half the chairs were filled, making it easy for Charlie and Kelsey to find seats next to each other.

"Is there anyone else?" Inez asked. Charlie had been coming here for years, and had never been able to put a finger on the moderator's age.

"Don't think so," they said. "It was pretty quiet on the way up."

"Then I think we'll begin," she said, now addressing the room. "I'd like to welcome everyone here tonight, and begin with a short, guided meditation to bring everyone into the moment. Get in a comfortable seated position, close your eyes, and follow my voice."

They obeyed, her voice in their ears. "Take this time to settle into yourself, to acknowledge where you are in this moment. Breathe deeply. Leave all other thoughts outside. The world will turn without them."

As Charlie inhaled and exhaled, they felt the work day and all the stresses it had brought, especially those of the morning's confrontation, fall away. The conversion was a bigger weight to lose, but things had been fairly quiet on that front since the community meeting.

They opened their eyes to a room of people with calmer faces. "Would anyone like to talk about what kind of a week you've been having?" Inez asked.

A few people spoke to tell stories about triumphs and setbacks that had recently taken place. Others, counselors and members alike, shared advice for rethinking similar situations so people didn't have to react this way in the future. Charlie listened to it all without feeling the need to say anything this time. They'd gotten through that disaster of an afternoon without any liquid help, they'd been too busy at the bar yesterday to even think about drinking more than their quick tastes, and their time with Justin was better than anything they could mix up. They didn't want to leave those thoughts outside the room. They wanted to dive deep into them and relive every magical moment until they could see him again.

"I think it's time for us all to go forward." Inez's voice broke into their thoughts. Where had the evening gone?

"Join hands, please. And remember..." She waited until the whole group was linked before speaking again. "You are stronger than you think, and capable of more than you can imagine. Hold onto that, and hold onto this shared energy as you leave this room and go into whatever lies ahead. Peace and strength to all of you."

Charlie felt the pressure of Kelsey's hand and that of the unknown man next to them, and returned the squeeze. The meeting had proven an excellent opportunity to recharge, and they felt ready for whatever lay ahead, both the bad—the condo conversion—and the good—what was forming with Justin.

****

While Janelle changed into a sundress after work, the restaurant she ultimately chose was casual enough that Justin could wear shorts to dinner without violating the dress code. All the same, he was glad they'd gotten a table inside. It had been brutally hot since he'd left Soho, and he'd spent the rest of the day hanging out in the air-conditioned apartment.

"Thanks for coming tonight," she said after the waitress left with their dinner orders. "I wanted to talk to you about the other day."

He put down his water glass and felt his spine stiffen. "Is this about what happened with Charlie?"

"It is, but not in the way you think." She sighed. "The whole thing made me think about how I've treated you this summer, and I'm sorry."

He was confused. "There's nothing to be sorry about. You let me take over your home office, you're not charging me rent—"

"And I've been infantilizing you the whole time," she finished. "I've been treating you like you're half your age—no, less than—and I feel bad about it. Because of that, I didn't know you were seeing Charlie."

"I didn't really tell anyone until ... you know," he said, thinking back. He'd only told a few work colleagues he was dating anyone at all, and he and

Charlie had been too busy trying and failing to consummate whatever was growing between the two of them to discuss what it actually was.

"Because I didn't exactly invite confidence, and I wish I'd been better about that. You're my brother, we're living together for the summer, and yet I hardly know you."

The waitress brought their dinners and gave Justin a bit of a break to process everything Janelle was telling him. "Well, what do you want to know?" he asked when she stepped away.

"About your internship, for starters. How's that going?"

"Pretty well." The conversation was stiff to start, but loosened a little as the meal went on. He told her about his department and the projects the firm was working on, Janelle shared anecdotes from her own jobs and internships, and the evening slowly fell away. While she wasn't as easy to talk to as Charlie—then again, who was?—she still had some interesting experiences and good advice to share.

"I'm glad we got to do this," she said as she signed the check.

"Me too. Thanks for inviting me." The two of them might never be super-close, but his sister was taking steps toward feeling more like a peer than a parental figure. He welcomed it.

Chapter Sixteen

"What are you doing tomorrow?" Justin asked Charlie. He'd slept late and taken one of the latest dinner slots of the night so he could meet them after work, and the thought had buoyed them through the rush of Saturday night. Now Lena was gone, having left for Ryan's after the kitchen had closed. Janelle was finishing up with the evening's receipts upstairs, and he was sitting across from them at the bar.

"I'm coming in to work in the afternoon, but my morning's free." That raised the question of what could happen in that time. The brunch scene near their place was a madhouse that they wanted no part of, but what alternatives were there?

Suddenly, a wonderful idea occurred to them. "Want to go on a hike with me?"

Justin frowned. "Where would we be doing this? I'm not much of a nature person."

"That's okay. Neither am I. The bugs, the poison ivy and brambles, peeing in the woods … no thanks." They shuddered at the memory of the itchiness, sore muscles, and soaked, stinking socks that had come after every forced march they'd endured as a scout. "No, we wouldn't have to leave the city for this."

"Then I'm intrigued. What time should I meet you?"

"The earlier we leave, the less crowded this'll be, not to mention the less hot. So maybe it'd be easier if you stayed the night."

He smiled. "I can do that. Let me just text my sister, and we can leave whenever."

"You can tell her if you want. She's upstairs."

"Okay." He headed up the stairs and knocked on the office door. Janelle opened it, and he spoke to his sister for a little while before coming back down to meet Charlie. She stood at the top of the stairs and watched the pair of them leave hand in hand with an unreadable expression, but they didn't dwell on it. After all, they were too preoccupied with the thought of what they wanted to do with Justin once they were back in the privacy of their apartment. The return to the work week had kept them both too busy to see each other for days, and sexy texts weren't cutting it.

The subway was too crowded with bar hoppers and club kids for either one of them to get a seat, but Justin gripped a pole with one hand and wrapped his free arm around them to keep them upright. They leaned into him and were rewarded by his hard chest and a stronger stirring below their waist. The pose brought back memories of the night of the Fourth, but he hadn't been lightly massaging their shoulder then. They pressed their ass into his thigh as they reached up and traced their fingertips over his hand.

He kissed the top of their head, and they all but melted into him. Naturally they were raging with heat and eager to be with him again, but the warmth that spread through them at this gesture was an entirely different animal. They couldn't remember the last time anyone had touched them with such tenderness.

After a few minutes of standing like that, he clasped their hand and turned them around to face him. "How many more stops?"

They glanced over his shoulder at the display before wrapping their arms around him. "Two, and then a bit of a walk."

"Good. I'm going crazy here." He leaned into them. His erection confirmed the truth of that statement and drove them wild, too.

A number of people got off at the next stop, but

Charlie stayed put and grinded their hips against him. "Once I get you upstairs…"

He pressed into them and growled with frustration and yearning. Given their own desires, they couldn't say they blamed him. Fortunately, the train pulled into their stop a short time later. They picked up the pace and led him down every shortcut they knew of to get home, but it was still taking too long.

After they finally unlocked the door, they all but backed Justin into it as they embraced him. He didn't seem to care, but kissed them back with enthusiasm. The height difference could seriously crick both their necks if they kept this up for long, so they raised one leg to hook around his waist. He lifted them up without breaking the kiss, and they wrapped both legs around him. This guy was *good*, and they weren't just thinking that because he'd placed them groin-to-groin with him. What exactly had he learned at that ballet school?

Through the kisses, the two of them pressed into each other the same way as at Helga's that day. But Willow was the only one around to judge this time, and they didn't even know where she was. At the moment, all they could think about was the sweetness of his tongue against theirs and the exquisite agony of the layers of clothing that acted as a barrier.

Justin stiffened and pulled away a bit. "I'm gonna come in my pants if you keep this up," he warned them.

Indeed, he looked like he was barely holding back, and the sight gave Charlie a thrill. Their eyes locked on his as they unhooked their legs and stood before him. "So take 'em off."

He didn't break their glance as he undid his belt and then the fly on his shorts, then yanked off all the clothes on his lower body. They carefully folded the clothes for something soft to kneel on in front of him, ran their fingertips over the dark stubble while lavishly licking their lips, and then traced the tip of his cock over the now-slick surface before taking him all the way into their mouth.

Justin gasped and rested his palm on the back of their head. Remembering something he'd told them, they reached a hand around to tease the area between his ass cheeks as they sucked him. He seemed to swell even further at the pressure, and they didn't stop their hand or mouth until he pulled them closer and came with a strangled yell. They tightened their lips around him and squeezed his ass.

"Oh, God, Charlie." Justin looked down at them with glazed eyes. "You…"

"I think I can imagine." Something had released in them as he'd come in their mouth, and they reached for his hand to show him the effect he'd had on them.

He stroked their palm with his thumb, then shed his shirt. Once he was totally naked, he lifted them with no effort and carried them to the bedroom. "Until I get hard again…"

They wanted to ask what he had in mind, but he answered their question by removing their shirt and kissing their eyelids, earlobe, and lips before moving to that spot on their neck that drove them wild. Then he traced his fingers over their chest and torso, and the lightest touch of his lips and tongue soon followed. Through it all, they barely felt the mattress under their back, just shivers and thrills from entirely unexpected sources.

It was such a relief when Justin unbuttoned their pants and took off the last of their clothes, but he didn't dive right in. Instead, he massaged their thighs up and down before kissing and licking their inner thighs, stopping not even an inch away from where they were feeling every touch. They couldn't decide whether to scream with desperation to take things further or tell him not to even think about stopping what he was doing.

He brushed his fingers just at the tip of their entrance, but didn't go in. "You feel ready for me."

As Justin's hands continued to work magic, Charlie reflected on every minute they'd ever spent hating their body. But after all the pleasure it had given them and someone else tonight—a shiver rippled through them as he hit a particularly sweet spot—everything was forgiven, if only for the moment.

****

A hand on his bare shoulder nudged Justin out of a deep sleep. He wasn't about to ask why he hadn't been visited by flashbacks to the accident in the past few weeks, but maybe he already knew. Maybe the endorphins generated by sex with Charlie were an antidote to the poisonous thoughts that had visited him all too often.

Then again, if a few fucks were what it took to get over this, he would have been cured years ago. Maybe they themself were the antidote. Before he'd even gotten in bed with them, and even when they hadn't gotten to do it, his days were happier and leading to more peaceful nights. He'd spent the past few years consumed with the idea that he'd lost everything, but it was becoming clear that he'd found something, namely some*one* he never would have if he'd stayed in Boston.

A kiss on the back of his neck scattered his thoughts and sent his eyes flying open. He turned over and smiled to see them already dressed and leaning over him. "What a way to wake up," he said, tracing a hand over their cheek.

Charlie grinned and leaned into his touch. "We ought to get going soon. It's gonna be another hot one, but we should avoid the worst of it now."

"Then I won't be long." He threw the covers back as he rose.

The cool of the room reminded him how the two of them had collapsed into bed naked after last night, and their face lit up to remind him what he wasn't wearing. "Or, you know what, we don't have to leave right this second. If there's anything you wanted to do before we go out—"

He pulled them back onto the bed with him. They pulled their t-shirt off with one hand and reached into the nightstand drawer with the other. He palmed the packet, unbuttoned their shorts, and lightly massaged them over their underwear as he kissed their chest. They shed their last layers, and he sucked a finger before sliding it inside them. He would never have danced with a *pas* partner without warming up, after all, and he didn't put the condom on until they were slick and ready for him.

This time, they climbed on top, but he wasn't about to make them do all the work. He raised his hips along with them. Charlie adjusted their position a few inches until they found an angle that changed their expression, and he didn't take his hands off them. Their moans fueled his own desire, and his own orgasm came shortly after theirs. They didn't climb off right away, but bent down to hold him close. He wrapped his arms around them, not wanting to put a stop to the moment any more than they did.

About an hour later, the two of them were dressed and getting off the subway. "So where are we hiking to, anyway?" Justin asked on the street.

Charlie stopped. "Brooklyn." The pedestrian entrance to the bridge stretched behind them. Despite the relatively early hour, several joggers and bikers were already out.

The two of them stepped on the path and headed across. With every step they took, more of the river and skyline came into view with the sun sparkling across every surface.

"Have you ever done this before?" he asked as the path took the two of them over the water.

"A few times, but it's been a while. You?"

"The school took some of us as an orientation activity when I first moved here, but I wasn't part of it. I've seen more of the city in the past month or so than the entire three years I lived here."

As he spoke, he realized the truth of it. The whole time he'd been at school, he'd barely left the blocks surrounding his Upper West Side campus. Now he could see Brooklyn to his left and a dramatically changed downtown skyline to his right. In either direction, the sun sent sparkles flying off the East River, where he also noticed the Statue of Liberty.

The more Justin walked, the more he realized the truth of their invitation. Walking across the Brooklyn Bridge wasn't unlike going on a hike. True, he heard car horns instead of bird calls, but he was still getting exercise. It was good to be outside instead of shut up in a gym or studio.

Only one thing would make the day more beautiful.

"What?" Charlie asked, stopping at his side as he paused.

"Just wanted to do this." He drew them close, and their lips found his. No one in this crowd knew him or them, and everyone seemed too intent on going on with the day to care about two people kissing in the middle of the Brooklyn Bridge.

After the two of them broke apart, Justin kept their hand in his for the rest of the walk across the bridge.

It was a gorgeous day, if a little hot, there was so much excitement happening beneath the skyline's façade, he was with someone he was coming to care about… The more time he spent here, the less he wanted to give it up.

Once the two of them stepped off in Brooklyn, he forced himself to bring up what had been moving from the back of his mind to the forefront over the past few days. "So now what are we going to do?"

"Get some water and maybe lunch, for starters," Charlie said. "Then I have to change before work, and you still have the full day ahead of you to do whatever you want, but we could make a plan for Monday night or sometime Tuesday."

"As good as that sounds, that's not what I mean."

They frowned. "I know. I know you'll have to go back to college soon."

"And it's not exactly close. If I wasn't staying with Janelle, I'd be looking at a commute of more than an hour each way to get to work."

"Ugh." They made a face that suggested they knew how onerous that would be.

The two of them walked in silence for a while before Charlie spoke again. "Well, when does the next semester start?"

"End of August." It wouldn't be for another five or six weeks, but it suddenly felt way too soon.

"Then that gives us more than another month. We don't have to decide anything right now, so we can just take things a day at a time. Make the most of it."

He smiled. "I can do that."

As he walked with Charlie, he reflected that this wasn't unlike the time a ballet company from San Francisco had done a temporary residency and he'd hit it off with one of their dancers. He and Lily had both known the arrangement was only for a few months before they returned to opposite sides of the country, but that hadn't stopped him from savoring every moment with her. And right now, he wanted to savor every moment with Charlie in their bedroom, in Brooklyn, and everywhere in between.

Chapter Seventeen

It was safe to say that Charlie approached that Monday morning in much better spirits than most of New York. While almost everyone was going back to work after the weekend, they'd been working through all of it and had their days off ahead of them.

Of course, the past few weeks had held happier workdays than they'd had in months, and they had Justin to thank for that. Weeks of colorful fantasy had recently turned into beautiful memories, and it wasn't over yet. The sooner they got to work, the sooner the day would end and they'd see him again tonight.

That was the thought that pushed them out of bed and into getting ready for work. They'd spent too much time luxuriating in the flashbacks to their time with him, and now they had just enough time to toss some food in a bowl for Willow and shower in a hurry. Once they were decent, they grabbed the stack of mail that had piled up over the past few days, stuffed it in their bag, and raced for the subway station.

When they changed trains at 34th Street, they were pleasantly surprised to see Lena on the subway. "Imagine running into you here," they said.

"Good morning to you, too," she said. "It was greenmarket day, so I thought I'd stop in before work."

"Good haul?" they asked. The small mountain of reusable bags at her feet made it a rhetorical question.

The subway pulled into the stop nearest Helga's, and they picked up some of Lena's bags.

"Careful with that one. There are eggs in there," she said, rising and glancing at the blue bag as she gathered up a handful of her own. "I was going to scramble some of them for breakfast before work. Care to join me?"

"Sure!" There had been no time to stop by the bakery this morning.

After unlocking the front door to the restaurant, Lena put fresh bread in the toaster before hefting out a large frying pan, turning the stove on low, and melting some butter and oil. Then she cracked the eggs in a bowl, whipped them with heavy cream, and finally poured the mixture in the pan. She didn't turn up the heat, but stirred the eggs with utmost concentration.

Charlie knew from experience that the eggs Lena made this way would take a while, but the end result would ultimately be worth the wait. They sat at a table, pulled out the stack of mail and looked through it. Some of this could be thrown out without a second thought— how many times would that no-imagination Chinese place send a menu before it got the message that they weren't interested?—but the official-looking letter demanded their attention.

Charlie sliced it open with the knife by their place. This note was briefer than the one announcing the conversion, but no less ominous for it. It listed a buyout amount and a deadline for when they would have to accept it or be out on the street. They didn't know much about real estate, but even they knew that while this looked like a lot of money, it wouldn't be enough to make a down payment on an apartment in the new building or anywhere else near them.

Lena turned off the stove and put the eggs on plates with toast, but Charlie's stomach was now too knotted to eat. The Fourth of July weekend had been a holiday in all senses, but now everyone, including the developer and landlord, was evidently back from vacation and raring to get back to work. That meant they'd better get to work, too, on finding a new place, but they had no idea where to start.

Lena took a few bites of her breakfast before noticing that they hadn't touched their plate. "What is it?" she asked.

"Message from management."

Lena took the letter. Her eyes narrowed a little more with every line. "This is seriously the best they can do?"

"But I can't afford to buy anything or rent someplace decent with this," they admitted miserably.

"No one can." She pulled out her phone. "Ryan just closed on his apartment and should still be in touch with the lawyer—I'll get the number so they can look this over and see if you're getting a fair deal. His broker was really good, too, if you want to talk to one."

"Thanks." Charlie felt a bit of relief and a flash of déjà vu to when they'd started working with Lena and she'd been so confident and take-charge. They might be living on the other end of the city by the time this was all over, but some things would never change.

That evening, Ryan stopped by the bar after his shift in the park. There was still a hint of stubble on his face, but his dark hair was damp from a shower and he was wearing dark shorts and a white shirt that accented his arm and leg muscles. Meeting him during that blizzard had made him look like a hot version of the Abominable Snowman, and he'd cleaned up even better since then. Charlie had been a little jealous that he'd gone for Lena instead of them, but it was funny how they hadn't even thought about that in weeks. They suspected a certain former dancer had something to do with it.

He sipped a glass of ice water as he texted them the contact information for his lawyer and broker. "Barb was really helpful through the process, and I'm still in touch with Joel." He grinned as Charlie's phone buzzed to indicate that they'd received his message. "Hard to believe I have a lawyer now."

"Sounds almost like being a grown-up, doesn't it?" They still couldn't believe they were in a position to have to worry about such things. It was heady at some times and scary at others, rather like now.

Their phone buzzed to remind them of the message. "Thanks for your help. I just wish there was another way."

Ryan's face clouded a bit. "I can't recommend that you get money for a down payment the way I did."

The reminder put Charlie to shame, and they put their hand on top of Ryan's. "I didn't even think. Fine way to thank you for your help, and I'm sorry."

He shook his head as if to clear it. "You didn't do anything wrong. Sometimes it just creeps up on me, but I don't want it to. It's a nice night, and I don't want to ruin it."

They smiled. "We got some new craft beers that might help with that."

Ryan smiled back, listened to their descriptions, and made his choice. The awkward moment was over, but Charlie's mind was still buzzing from it as they poured his drink. For one thing, Ryan had clearly had a much better relationship with his parents than they did with their own. For another, it was clear that he hadn't been a New Yorker for long. Otherwise he'd know that this wasn't just about seeing the structure go down. Losing the building where they'd lived all those years would mean losing the life they'd built up in the neighborhood, and it would be a kind of death.

****

The day was already blazing hot, but Justin didn't feel it as he got off a subway stop early and walked the rest of the way to work. Either he was in better shape than he thought, or the joy of his time with Charlie was generating so many endorphins that he didn't feel anything.

And as he was seeing them again tonight, he was sure to generate more. He swiped his pass like he'd been working there for years and took the elevator up, ready to start but already counting down to the end of the day at the same time.

"Good weekend, huh?" Denise asked as she sat down.

His smile widened. "Great. The whole city was great, to be honest. So much to see, and Helga's had some great things on the menu."

She smiled ruefully as her shirt brushed against a streak of sunburnt skin. "And to think I spent my weekend frying in the Hamptons again."

"Maybe another time." His computer had fully booted up by now, and he looked back at it. "So where should I start? Tribeca again?"

"No, I think we're at a pretty good stopping place with that one for now, but we could move on to having you do more with the Lower East Side project. The developer just made a bunch of offers, and things can really move into gear once the last holdouts make arrangements to move out. And once they do, we want to be ready to go right away."

She sent him a link to a presentation, and Justin clicked through it with interest that grew as he looked more closely. The street address sounded vaguely familiar, as did the pictures of the buildings currently on the sites. He unlocked his phone and checked the address Charlie had given him all those weeks ago.

His stomach dropped as he realized their address fell right in the range of buildings marked for demolition. Did they know about this? What was going to happen to them? He resumed his work, but with a widening pit of dread forming in his stomach.

Before he knew it, Denise had left and Conor was dismissing him for the day. He walked to Helga's with less of a spring in his step than usual, greeted Ashley— he was starting to know the evening's hostesses by name—and looked for Charlie.

There they were, leaning over the bar and talking to a guy who looked like he could fit them in his pocket and bench-press the bar. They put their hand on top of his for a moment and said something before turning back to work.

Justin watched the whole scene with an unexpected burst of fury in his stomach. He'd never thought of himself as the jealous type, but seeing Charlie touch and lean in close to quite obvious competition had gotten his back up like none of his past hookups ever had.

"Who was that?" he asked, taking a seat a few stools down from the unknown man.

"Hello to you, too," Charlie said.

"Sorry. Hi." He tried to smile to soften his words. "But what was going on with that? Who was he?"

"My boss's boyfriend. He was giving me his lawyer and broker's contact information because I'm going to have to move, and it brought back some uncomfortable memories."

"Oh." The explanation helped, but didn't wash away his reaction or his surprise at having it. Worst of all, their move didn't sound like a coincidence in light of what he'd learned at work.

They cocked their head. "Are you sure you're okay?"

He sighed. "Yeah, it's just that my evaluation's coming up next week. It's part of the internship program, and we used to have to do similar things in school and at the company, but that doesn't mean I'm looking forward to it."

"Sounds like a body wax to me—one flash of pain and then it's all over." They squeezed his hand. "But seriously, it sounds like you have this in the bag. I know how hard you work. I know you're treating this like a real job and not one of the stupid summer activities I always got pushed into. As long as—who's doing this?"

"The head of the company. I've barely seen him since I started. I work more closely with his underlings." Denise, one of said underlings, had dropped that bomb at the end of the day, and it seemed as good a reason for a bad mood as any. The knowledge of what was happening to their building also weighed on him, and he didn't want to bring it up if he could avoid it.

"Well, as long as they've told him about that, you'll be fine."

He returned the squeeze. "Thanks."

The pose was almost identical to the one he'd walked in on, and they stroked the top of his hand with their thumb as they spoke. "You don't have to worry about your evaluation, and you do *not* have to worry about Ryan. Believe me, he has eyes for no one but Lena."

"I didn't—"

The look on Charlie's face told him they weren't fooled for a minute. "I'll give you some support if you're having a bad day at my bar, but I don't do this with all my patrons."

They leaned as far as they could over the bar. Justin figured out what they were up to, leaned forward, and met their lips. The kiss calmed some of the suddenly roiling feelings and ended all too soon.

"And I don't let just anyone in on my secrets." They turned their back, squeezed some lemon juice into a shaker, and added a few more ingredients before serving him a drink in a frosted glass.

He frowned. "I shouldn't."

"I know, you said you wanted to cut back on alcohol. And this doesn't have any."

He took a sip to be sure, and was pleasantly surprised. "Still good."

"One of my own creations," they said proudly. "I don't want to just sip a club soda for the rest of my life."

A crowd of people dressed similarly to him in his early days at the internship arrived, and Charlie left to take care of them. All Justin could do was sip his drink and reflect on the unexpected turn the evening had taken. Why had he reacted like that when he'd walked into the bar? And how were they going to take it when they found out where he was working?

Chapter Eighteen

Charlie stirred as Justin crawled out of bed. "I have to get going," he whispered.

The light pouring in under the blinds told them the sun hadn't been up that long. "It's so early," they protested.

"I want to put on a suit for work," he said. "I'll see you tonight."

They leaned into the touch of his lips and the pressure of his hands on their shoulders. The stress of his upcoming review had killed Justin's libido last night, but that was not to say it hadn't been nice to have him with them. The two of them had gotten under the covers together after watching a movie on the bed. Charlie had fallen asleep quickly, but not without noticing how well they fit against him and how cherished they felt in his arms.

As he slipped out the door, Charlie wrapped the blanket tighter around their shoulders. His warmth had evaporated all too soon, and the air around them was uncomfortably cool. Even Willow doing her impression of a space heater wasn't enough to warm the rest of the bed.

A few hours later, when they decided to get up for the day and feed Willow, Charlie pulled on a t-shirt, pair of pajama pants, and socks to stay warm in the room where their air conditioner was now freezing them out. At the same time, they knew leaving it off too long would make the apartment unlivable. In other words, it was another one of *those* summer days in New York.

There was nothing else for it. They turned off the air conditioner, had a quick, cool shower and shave to try to regulate their body temperature, and then reached into the back of their closet to dig out an airy blue sundress with a pattern of tiny white flowers. It was the best option for a day like this. They felt better already and welcomed the prospect of not spending the whole day with their skin suffocated.

They dropped some ice cubes in Willow's water dish before leaving for the afternoon. After checking emails over an iced coffee, they walked to the salon they'd been visiting from the time they'd moved in. The heat pressed on their bare skin all the while, but they silently rejoiced in the breezes that snuck in under their arms and skirt, not to mention the freedom to wear whatever they wanted whenever the mood struck them. Everyone around here was too busy to keep track of what they were wearing from day to day or to bother them about it. As if to prove their point, a man with bright pink hair and a pair of tiny hairless dogs on leashes walked by without attracting a second glance.

An hour later, they were looking in a mirror at a tidied-up haircut. "You like?" the petite hairdresser asked.

"Very much." What was not to like? Their hair looked great, the look had perked up their eyes and face, and they were extremely relaxed from a stronger shoulder and scalp massage than they would have expected from such a girl even tinier than they.

They paid at the register, clasped a tip into her hand, and walked a few blocks west for lunch at one of their favorite cafés. Sawasdee Amigos was a Thai-Mexican fusion restaurant run by a husband and wife team who could have stepped out of a sitcom, and they went for the food almost as much as for the atmosphere.

"Are you ready?" Maria asked.

"Yeah, I'll have the tacos with chicken and pineapple, please."

A shout of triumph erupted from behind the

kitchen. "I told you the pairing would work!" Somchai shouted as his wife ran their credit card.

Maria rolled her eyes. "Yeah, well, you'll understand my skepticism after the eggplant debacle!"

As the two owners bantered, Charlie took a number from the counter and carried it to a table by a window facing the park. There they enjoyed the sight of people walking past with babies, dogs, friends, and partners. Sawasdee Amigos was yet another new restaurant that had sprung up around here over the past few years … when neighborhood rents were still low and an exciting young upstart, as an early review had called Helga's, could afford to open up in Manhattan.

Unwelcome thoughts of the conversion wormed back into their head. They could always take the subway here to keep getting their hair cut and visiting their favorite places, but how much longer would these places last in the face of these new condos and a newly moneyed crowd? The very thought of everything good being priced out and national chains muscling the way in made them sick.

A waiter came over bearing a plate of three fragrant tacos and a small side of chips and pineapple salsa. The Thai-spiced chicken made their mouth water, but their stomach was clenched too tightly for them to eat it. They tried to comfort themself with the thought that maybe they could move into a place with central air conditioning, but it didn't help.

****

Justin straightened his tie. Lately he'd been coming to work dressed more casually, like his colleagues, and he'd gotten way too used to it. Nevertheless, he thought it best to put on a suit for the evaluation.

"Justin?" Conor said. "Mr. Herrera is ready for

you."

He stood and knocked at his ultimate boss's door. "Come in. Have a seat," Bernardo Herrera said.

He entered the office and sat facing the man who'd ultimately agreed to hire him, the man who'd been at the helm of every opening he'd gotten to attend thus far, yet whom he'd barely spoken to since he started work.

"Yes, sir."

The tall Hispanic man pulled up a file on his computer. "Well, Justin, you've been here for a little over a month. How would you say things are going so far?"

One of *those* interviews. Justin chose his words carefully so as not to hand him any ammunition. "So far, I feel like I've learned a lot about the process of building in New York City. I have a good team to work with— that always helps—and it's been good to see how the little things I do play into the greater goal."

"And Conor and Denise agree," Bernardo said. "They both told me you seemed a little unsure to start out with, but that you learned quickly and were soon able and eager to take on new tasks and more responsibility. They had nothing but good things to say about your work. Therefore, I have nothing but good to say about your internship, but I do want to ask you a question."

Justin sat up a little straighter. "Yes?"

"Is this something you think you'd like to continue with?"

He answered the question with one of his own. "How do you mean?"

"While working here would certainly be a possibility, I don't want to make any promises. I do want to know if you like what you've been doing and think you'd like to keep it up."

"Definitely, sir."

Bernardo sat back. "Remind me again what your major is."

"English, sir, but my time here has me thinking of switching to architecture."

"Then how did you decide to come here?"

"I used to be a professional ballet dancer until I got hurt. After my injury, I realized that as good as our dancing was, it didn't tell the whole story. The sets could really make or break a show." All true, but this was neither the time nor place to mention his flings with the guys in the crew.

"So you see architecture as a form of world building." Bernardo nodded thoughtfully. "If you like what you've been doing here, I would encourage you to add some art or engineering classes to your curriculum as well as the usual architecture major. That would really make a difference in showing you how to create your own worlds and setting you up for this as a career path."

He nodded. "Okay."

"Good." Bernardo sat back at his desk. "Now I have a meeting to prepare for, and you have more work to do today. But when I get back, I'm going to want you to take a more active hand in the Lower East Side project."

Justin headed back to his desk, his mind racing too much to concentrate on the day ahead. It was such a relief that his review had gone so well, and highly gratifying to have an esteemed architect tell him he had a future in his newly chosen field.

On the other hand, he didn't know what to say or do about the Lower East Side project. What was Charlie going to say when they found out?

Then again, did they even need to know? The review had taken place at his internship's halfway mark, and he didn't remember them objecting to it. Could he make it to the end of the summer without bringing this up?

Chapter Nineteen

Charlie sighed as they clicked through real estate listings online. One tab had sales, another had rentals, and all showed how much things had changed since they'd first moved to New York. If they wanted to stay around here in an apartment like the one they lived in now, poor lighting and all, they would need a lot more than the buyout offer was giving them. But if they wanted to keep paying what they did in rent, they'd have to move to the depths of Brooklyn or some part of Queens they couldn't find on a map. Either way would take forever to get to work.

It didn't help to see that for what they had saved, they could buy a mansion in Kansas and lord their success over everyone who'd been mean to them growing up. They couldn't just pack up and leave their job, their friends, their community … the whole life they'd built up in New York.

Charlie's chest clenched as they pushed away from their laptop and glanced around the room. Even if they did find a place in an area they liked, how were they going to schlep eleven years of life from one end of town to the other? The thought of choosing what to keep and toss, and then packing up this entire apartment and moving it someplace else overwhelmed them.

Willow rubbed against their leg, her fur silken against their bare skin. Instead of being comforted, the gesture reminded them that once they found a place that would let them bring her, they'd have to move there with her. After the adoption, the most they'd ever traveled with her was putting her in her carrier for a walk to the vet's office. Who knew how she'd act in a taxi or on the subway?

The buzzer went off to jerk them out of these

worries and remind them that they were seeing Justin tonight. They closed all the windows in their browser and frowned at their reflection. The search had made them look too pinched and worried, but they couldn't leave him sweltering outside while they tried to work a makeup miracle. So instead of going downstairs, they sent him a text. **Still getting ready, but come on up.**

He was in good enough shape that the climb up the flights of stairs hadn't winded him, yet his breath caught at the sight of Charlie. They grinned as he stopped short. "Hi."

"Hey. I've never seen…"

They'd almost forgotten what they were wearing in the stress of the search, but grinned as he stumbled. "It's funny … once the pressure to wear dresses all the time was off, I realized I didn't mind putting one on every now and then."

"Well, it works. You look great."

"Thanks. Don't get used to it, though. Remember, it all depends on how I'm feeling." Past experiences and expectations from parents and former partners alike tempered their present response to the compliment on them in the dress.

"I get it." Justin raised his hand in mock surrender. "You keep me on my toes."

He wrapped his arms around them and kissed them lightly, adding, "And I like that."

Pleasantly flustered, and having forgotten all about the search, Charlie kissed him back before reluctantly disengaging. "Well, that's one way of putting it. Do you mind just waiting a few minutes while I finish getting ready?"

"Not at all."

"Thanks. Make yourself comfortable. I'll try not to be too long."

AN ESPECIALLY HOT SUMMER

Charlie closed the bathroom door behind them and got out some supplies. The sight of Justin had softened their expression a bit, but they could still do better than this. A few strokes of concealer and blush would make their skin more even and radiant, exactly as they wanted to look for him.

He looked up as they came out. "Are you ready?"

"'Fraid not. My bathroom lighting doesn't work for this, and no shirt, no *shoes*, no service, remember?" He smiled, and they added, "I won't be much longer."

Back in the bedroom, Charlie faced the mirror and set to work. Another dab of the concealer stick, another swipe of the blush brush, and they leaned down to dig around in their closet for a pair of sandals they hadn't worn much yet this year. They found the shoes under a pile of promotional tote bags, but the scene out the door kept them from disrupting it. Willow had come out to see Justin surveying the room from the couch, and she was nuzzling the hand he'd extended to her. He reached out to pet her head, and she didn't move away.

Something softened in the center of their chest. All this time they'd known how they felt about him, but the euphoria of the first dates, the first times had a way of blinding them to potential red flags and sending them into relationships with people who didn't always deserve them or their time. That was where Willow came in. People who ignored her or nudged her away didn't last much longer, and they were glad to see that Justin wasn't in either category. He was passing their test with flying colors.

They stepped further away from the door where they couldn't possibly be seen. He was still absorbed in petting the cat, but they still didn't want to spoil the surprise.

****

CHELLE DE NOTTE

As he waited for Charlie, Justin realized that in all the times he'd been to their place, he'd never actually seen it. He was too interested in what he could do in the bedroom with them to look at its décor. He'd also barely glanced at the bathroom, and had always been too distracted to notice the living room.

Now that he was alone in here, he glanced around the living room. Half the window was occupied by an air conditioning unit, but it didn't keep light from streaming in. He looked out it to the street and saw similar rowhouses, shops, and restaurants in what looked like a set from an old-time movie. The memory of the sketches of the new glass building nagged at him, and he couldn't imagine how such a thing was going to fit in around here.

To put the thought out his mind, he returned to the firm couch and looked around the living room. A lightweight throw was on the back of the couch, and a few magazines were scattered across the coffee table. Across the room, a small patch of cat grass sat on a low shelf near the window. Behind him, the kitchen was small but spotless, save for a stack of mail on the counter.

The whole place was about half the size of Janelle's, but had more of a sense of home and permanence than hers did. His heart clenched at the thought of them losing it. Where were they going to go next? How were they going to recreate this somewhere else? And what would be harder—telling them who he was working for, or keeping it a secret?

A light thump distracted him, and he looked up. Charlie's cat had jumped up on the couch next to him. It had mostly made itself scarce on his previous visits, but had come out more often and was now regarding him with skepticism.

Justin wasn't entirely used to pets. Both his

parents' allergies had precluded a dog or cat when he was growing up, and Janelle lived in a no-pets building. Some of the principals he'd worked with had dogs, but he couldn't imagine how the busiest people he knew had made time to take care of such a demanding pet. But none of that was to say he didn't like animals. On the contrary, he liked seeing and petting friendly dogs on the street. He didn't see cats as often, but admired their beauty and grace.

And Charlie's cat was certainly beautiful. This was the closest he'd ever seen her, aside from mornings when she was chirping for breakfast from the nightstand next to his head, and he admired her sleek shape. Her bright green eyes stood out vividly in an entirely dark gray coat.

He wasn't sure how to approach her, so he reached out his hand as he would to an unfamiliar dog. The cat sniffed it from a distance, then stepped a little closer. He slowly, awkwardly petted her head, marveling at how soft her fur was. She leaned in a little closer and rubbed her face against his hand.

Charmed, he ran his hand over her head and back. She stepped closer, kneaded his thigh with her front paws, and lay down on his leg. He stroked the cat with the realization that she was as sweet as he would have expected of any pet owned by Charlie. The thought of them warmed his heart as much as the cat's affection, but also nagged at his conscience. He didn't know how to tell them and didn't want to lose them.

"You little traitor," they said as they left the bedroom.

He startled a bit at their words, but their smile and glance down told him they were talking to their cat. "She won't move, but I don't care."

They sat next to him on the sofa. Instead of

clambering over him to be with her owner, Willow stayed where she was. "Scratch behind her ears. She likes that," they suggested.

They made a scratching motion in the air, and Justin followed their lead. Sure enough, it sounded exactly like someone had turned up the volume on the cat's purrs. He grinned. "She's really cute."

Charlie stroked her back. "And she's exactly what I needed."

"What do you mean?"

"I adopted her when I was in the early days of recovery. Kelsey had just gotten Bandit from the shelter, and she said, 'If you can't or won't keep it together for yourself, do it for her.' I'm not saying that was the magic key that made everything all better all at once, but it was a big help and something to think about before going off the deep end." They smiled. "Not to mention no one on my floor has had a mouse problem since I brought her home."

Justin grimaced. "So you had one before?"

"Remember those Craigslist roommates I mentioned? One of them wasn't familiar with the concept of cleaning up after himself in the kitchen, and I don't think I have to draw you a picture." They sighed. "Is it any wonder I was so glad to reach a point where I didn't have to advertise for roommates anymore?"

Justin felt worse with every word. He tried to smile, but it must have looked more like a grimace, because they asked, "Are you okay?"

He squeezed their thigh to reassure them. "It's been a long day."

The two of them sat in silence before Charlie stood up and shook some dry cat food into a bowl. Willow shot off the couch and into the kitchen, and they smiled after her.

"I'm not above resorting to bribery. If she didn't move, we wouldn't get dinner until midnight."

"It's fine." His stomach was so knotted up with guilt about his internship that he didn't know how much room he'd have for food.

Chapter Twenty

Charlie took another bite of their omelet and glanced around the restaurant, feeling happier and more relaxed than they had since their scalp massage. The comfortable atmosphere, homelike crowd, and delicious meal always calmed them, and today it assured them that this place at least would be safe from whatever gentrification had in store.

The setting sun filled the room with a soft glow that beautifully backlit Justin and filled them with further contentment. While it wasn't likely that they'd get to take him to all their favorite places, they were glad they'd gotten to bring him here tonight. It was all too clear that the summer was winding down, but they didn't want to think about that now. They just wanted to stay in the moment, as Kelsey and Inez constantly advised.

"How's your food?" they asked.

He picked up another fry and ate it with the dutiful expression of a child who'd promised to take a certain number of bites. "Delicious. Why?"

"You're just so quiet tonight," they said. Then they remembered. "Oh yeah, your review was today, right? How'd it go?"

"Better than I thought." He smiled with pride. "Everyone's really happy with my work—"

"As they should be," they interjected.

"And at the very least, I'm assured of a solid letter of recommendation."

"That's great!" They raised a glass of lemonade, and he clinked his water glass against it.

They took a sip of their drink and a look around the restaurant. "Then I'm doubly glad I got to bring you here tonight. Makes it like a celebration."

He smiled. "Thanks for that."

Now seemed like as good a time as any to tell him. "And there's one more thing we can do to celebrate."

"What?"

They leaned in close. "Well, I never wear anything on top to begin with. And while you were making friends with Willow, I took off my underwear."

Justin looked as if they'd announced that the Tuesday night in July was actually Christmas Eve. "So all evening, you've been..."

They nodded, unable to keep the devilish grin off their face. Both plates were practically empty, but he looked ravenous as he gestured to the waiter for the check. Charlie couldn't blame him. A throb of anticipation had been pulsing from their center all night long, and it was lucky they'd chosen a restaurant so close to their apartment.

As on the day they'd met him at what turned out to be Janelle's apartment, the two of them spent the walk home as models of composure. It wasn't easy for Charlie. The evening air had cooled from unbearably hot to the perfect temperature, and it felt delicious against every inch of their bare skin, especially under their skirt. The thought of his hands, mouth, or cock moving there spurred them on, and he had no trouble keeping up. But once their door locked behind them, the two of them didn't even wait to get to the bedroom before pressing into each other, running their hands all over each other's bodies and kissing in a frenzy.

As they untucked his shirt and ran their hands all over his bare skin, he slid a hand up their thigh, as if to prove to himself that they were telling the truth. "Damn, you're slick," he rasped, his thumb sliding over them.

"Because of you." They reached down to the shorts he'd changed into before coming to meet them, undid the fly, and slipped a hand into his boxer briefs. They could feel his pulse pounding through his hot, rock-solid cock, and the touch revved them up even further.

Charlie snarled with frustration and desire. "And all my condoms are in the bedroom."

"I bought more on the way over. They're in my bag."

They pulled away reluctantly and made their way to the other side of the room, where Justin had dropped a gym bag after he'd arrived for the evening. They pulled out the box, not to mention about half the bag's contents along with it in their eagerness.

"Shit." They hastily repacked the casual clothes and handful of protein bars, but something in a sheaf of spilled papers caught their eye.

As they looked again, the temperature of the room seemed to drop fifty degrees before shooting up to an uncomfortable heat. All the while, their desire died out as their stomach churned painfully. How long had this been going on? Why had he kept coming back to the bar? Was their entire summer a lie?

****

The longer Charlie was away from him, the crazier it drove Justin. Their announcement had been the only thought on his mind since leaving the restaurant, and he wanted nothing more than to act on the tsunami of need coursing through his body. He didn't even think he could wait to get undressed. He'd be more than happy to drop his pants, let them on his lap with that dress hiding everything, and go to town underneath it … if they'd only come back.

"Leave it," he begged. "I'll put it back later."

Charlie didn't reply or give any indication that they'd heard him. Doing his best to ignore his body's demands, he walked up behind them. "You okay?"

They faced him slowly with an expression of shellshock on their face. "Why do you have papers and folders from Bernardo Herrera's office?" Their tone and expression were neutral, but they couldn't keep a small tremor out of their voice.

Now that the moment of truth had come, there was nothing he could do but face it. "Because that's where I'm doing my internship."

They went rigid. "What?"

"I'm doing my internship at Bernardo Herrera's office," he said slowly. "You knew I was doing an internship with an architect when we met."

"Yeah, but not the architect who's going to replace my building when it's torn down!"

"Fuck." His erection shrank to nonexistence, and his voice could barely work. "Oh, fuck."

"And you knew about it?"

"Not until recently. Everybody in the office kept talking about the Lower East Side project, that's all anyone ever called it, but I didn't put two and two together on the addresses until pretty recently."

"And how recently is 'pretty recently'? Yesterday? Last week? Last month?" Their eyes narrowed. "Why did you come into Helga's that first day, anyway?"

"Because my sister works there, I told you."

"How convenient."

"What does *that* mean?"

"It means it let you go in without anyone thinking anything of it, and let you get close to someone in one of the buildings to tell your boss what I'm up to, how close I am to moving out, how close the buildings are to vacant so they can bulldoze my entire history in New York." Their eyes widened, then narrowed. "Is Bernardo Herrera the only one you're working for, or does the developer have a hand in this, too? Send in a nice piece of ass to get close to one of the holdouts?"

They were breathing hard by the end of this, and Justin took offense at their characterization. "Okay, that's just paranoid."

"So now I'm both paranoid and standing in the way of some grand vision. Thanks a lot."

"That's not what I mean, and you know it."

"Do I? I don't know what I know or who you are anymore."

Justin was stung. "I'm still me, and I still want you."

He leaned forward to touch their shoulder, and Charlie recoiled as if he'd come at them with a branding iron. "Don't touch me!"

He backed off. "Then what do you want me to do?"

"Answer me this: If I hadn't found out, would you ever have told me who you were working for? Or would you have just strutted back to school with another notch on your belt and the thrill of getting away with it?"

He hesitated. "I don't know."

Charlie's frown deepened. "That's what I thought."

"No! I don't know because I never got to find out, never got to figure out what to do about it." This was driving him crazy and doing nothing to improve his mood. "You know, you never even asked which architect I was working with. You just took my internship in stride and kept talking about you, you, you."

"Well, for someone who just talks about me, me, me, I sure asked a lot of questions about you when we were getting to know each other. You could've said something and not put this all on me for not doing a background check before I decided to sleep with you.

You're the one who took the internship—"

"Before I even knew you existed—" he had to interject.

"And then snuck around, trying to play both sides before anyone found out. Well, now that I know, what are you going to do?"

"What do you mean? I can't quit my internship. I can't walk away from the one thing I'd actually consider doing now that I can't dance anymore."

Their face darkened. "So you're just going to stick with it and not think about who you hurt in the process."

"I'm not doing this to hurt you or anyone."

"No, that's just what's happening as the result of your work."

They turned away. Justin tried to move into their line of sight, but they closed their eyes. "No. I can't even look at you now."

He sighed and picked up his gym bag. "Then I won't stick around. I'll get out of your way."

He closed the door behind them and headed for the subway. This was the most unbelievable evening he'd ever spent, and there was no right way out of it. Because he meant what he said up there: he couldn't quit his internship just over halfway in. Even if he never worked for the man again, a letter of recommendation with his name on it would go a long way in getting another architecture job, and he couldn't jeopardize his future now that it looked like he finally had one again. He'd thought part of caring about someone meant wanting the best for them, and he wasn't getting that vibe from Charlie now.

Charlie. The thought of the name was a punch to the gut, but he forced himself to keep walking. It wasn't like they were the love of his life. It wasn't like this thing could even go anywhere after he had to go back to college and they were working too hard to see him on weekends. Maybe it was even better that it had ended now, rather than leading to an incredibly uncomfortable conversation where neither of them would come out feeling good.

By the time he got to the subway, he had almost convinced himself of all of it. He'd go to work tomorrow, go about his summer as he'd planned before this, and go back to his regular life. And try to ignore the shard of pain that nagged at him like a splinter in his side.

Chapter Twenty-One

A sharp pain in their cheek yanked Charlie from a Benadryl-induced sleep. "*Hey!* What—"

They sat up sharply and threw the covers away from their face so as not to get blood on the sheets—how and why had Willow done that? Their shout sent her to the other side of the room, but it didn't tear her eyes from their face. She gave them an unblinking glare as she prowled back to the bed with the determination of her ancestors in the wild.

"Look, we both know it's too early for breakfast, and—" Their voice trailed off as they tried to remember what time they'd given her dinner last night. They couldn't, which led them to wonder if they had at all. "Oh baby, I'm sorry."

They dragged themself out of bed, headed to the kitchen, and gave Willow some extra food in her dish. Before she could eat it, they held her close to their chest. Kelsey had told them to keep their shit together for their pet at the very least, and they'd proven themself incapable of even that. "I'm so sorry."

She squirmed out of their grip and set to breakfast. Seeing her eating again assuaged their guilt a bit and let them crawl back under the covers, where they'd been since Justin's betrayal. They'd traded the airy dress for their warmest sweats to offset the chill that had taken root and taken a big dose of Benadryl to let them sleep and forget the questions swirling in their head. First, he hadn't thought to mention he was staying with his sister until she could have walked in on them, and now he hadn't mentioned that he was working for the designer of their building's replacement... How many secrets had Justin been keeping, and what else was he going to bring up only when it looked like he might get caught? How could they have been with someone so cagy?

Charlie had hoped they'd feel better after a good night's sleep, but they'd woken up the next morning feeling as rotten as before. They were still hurt by the news of Justin's internship, but a small, still voice had risen up to point out that they could have handled the discovery better. They'd taken another sedative dose to silence it and then two sick days of work, only getting out of bed to feed Willow and stop by the bathroom in all that time. The despair had been too crushing for them to move, never mind run a bar and restaurant.

As tempting as it would be to stay in bed for a few more days, the small voice reminding them of their own fault was growing louder and sending them into worse turmoil. Not to mention they couldn't leave Lena hanging on the weekend. That thought was the one that made Charlie drag themself up, clean the bite, take three days of the pill at once, and get in their first shower and shampoo since Tuesday morning. Once they were clean again, they chose a monochromatic outfit that would make them presentable without any thought. They were still a little groggy from all the antihistamines they'd taken to fall and stay asleep, so they went out for coffee.

"You okay, hon?" Angela asked before they could place an order.

"Yeah, why?" they asked.

"Only I wish I could get as pale as you are now without makeup."

"Don't eat for a few days and that'll do it," they mumbled.

She blinked a few times. "Come again?"

"I've been off food since Tuesday night." Showering wasn't the only thing that had fallen by the wayside in the aftermath of the fight.

Angela's elaborately lined eyes widened as she pulled out a chocolate doughnut with a blood red glaze, cut off a large chunk, and shoved it at them. "Okay, I was going to put this out as a sample anyway, but eat this before you pass out from low blood sugar."

She obviously didn't want a medical emergency in the bakery any more than Charlie would have liked one at the bar, and that compelled them follow her instructions. The sweet raspberry glaze burst on their tongue to revive them a little, and the dark chocolate doughnut seemed to flip a switch that woke them up all the way. "Thanks. I'll take one of these and a small coffee, please."

After stuffing a five-dollar bill in the tip jar, they sipped the coffee on the way to the subway and ate the full-sized doughnut on the ride uptown. All the while, they noticed that the further they got from their building, the more relieved they felt. Maybe hanging around the site of the fight had been a mistake from the start. Maybe getting away had been the answer all along.

Then again, maybe getting away to Helga's wasn't the best choice. After all, if Justin had gone anywhere else at all for drinks, they never would have met him. This was where they'd gotten to know him, arranged for the first dates, stolen kisses, gotten busted in the bathroom… They'd thought they were on the road to recovery after the trip to the bakery, but seeing this place sent them back to the abyss. Nevertheless, they squared their shoulders and forced themself to walk in.

Lena looked up from the stove and smiled as Charlie knocked on the kitchen door to say hello. "It's good to have you back. Feeling better?"

They forced a smile. "I'll live, but I'd better not hang around the bar today."

Lena frowned. "Shame. Melons are coming back

in season, and I know you could do something great with what I found this morning."

"Okay, I'll try them out when it's quiet, but I don't want to bartend too much."

"That's fine." She gave them a searching look. "What was wrong, anyway?"

"Nothing I want to go into here." It was amazing how much they could hide with one true statement, and how quickly Lena swallowed it while she was distracted with her new recipe. They headed upstairs to the office and gave silent thanks that Janelle had decided to take the day and weekend off.

True to their word, Charlie came downstairs between the lunch and dinner rushes to taste the watermelon and cantaloupe Lena had bought at the greenmarket. The sweetness of the melons woke up the sense of taste they brought to the bar and sparked their imagination.

Despite having to turn on their creativity, the whole day felt dull around the edges and as faded as if it had gone in the wash too many times. In an attempt to wake themself up, Charlie tried taking extra sips of the spiked melon punch they'd concocted. Part of them knew this was a dangerous thing to do, but a larger part couldn't be bothered to care.

As the city's typical workday ended and people started streaming in for happy hour, Charlie headed back up to the office. They couldn't stand the thought of seeing Justin again, not when they still felt so raw. They forced him aside to go over the paperwork that would have been Janelle's job.

They'd lost track of time when a waiter knocked on the door. "Lena wants to know if you want anything," he said.

They blinked, having not had any solid food

beyond the doughnut and fruit all day. An actual meal with protein and vegetables was probably a good idea, but they didn't know if they could force themself to choke it down. "I'll be right down. Thanks."

Charlie clung to the shadows as much as they could on the walk down. Justin wasn't at the bar, but they still didn't want to be seen. As they entered and stood at the edge of the kitchen, Lena looked up from the fragrantly spiced shrimp she was stirring at the stove. "What can I make you?" she asked.

"Nothing too heavy. I can't take much since that dinner on Tuesday."

"That dinner..." Her voice trailed off, and she looked closely at them. "Does this have anything to do with what's-his-face?"

The echo of their own words all those months ago drove another knife into their heart. "He's working for the architect who wanted to tear down my building, and we had a big blowout about it."

Lena's eyes widened. "Well, now I see why you wanted to stay away from the bar."

They glumly nodded.

The hiss of the shrimp demanded Lena's attention, but she turned back to them after removing the pan from the heat and passing the project off to another chef. "Want me to 'overcook' his dinner the next time he comes in?"

"No, it's better this way. It was never going to last. I shouldn't have let it get to me like that." They spoke to remind her as much as themself.

"But it did." There was no judgment in her dark eyes, just compassion. "I'm really sorry."

"Thanks." The acknowledgment extended to her words and the heirloom tomato-watermelon gazpacho she served them with a multigrain roll from Balthazar. It cleared their head and reminded them they still had people in their corner.

Back home, they unlocked the mailbox to find a thicker sheaf of envelopes than usual. Hardly surprising, seeing as they hadn't been near it since Tuesday night. They brought it up and mindlessly rifled through it. Bills … sales flyers … menus … and a letter from the bank.

The logo stirred them from their stupor, and they sliced the envelope open with a knife. A small mountain of paperwork explained their credit score, one higher than they would have expected, and the mortgages they would be eligible for.

Charlie set the letter down in a haze unlike the one they'd come to work in. Now they could really get going and get away. They'd spent so much time thinking they'd mourn the loss of their building, but now they thought they wouldn't mind seeing the site of bad memories bulldozed to the ground, blown up—At the moment, they didn't care how it would happen so long as it would be gone.

****

The audience made approving sounds as Justin leaped in the center of the admiring party guests. But instead of going into his next variation, he landed in a way that snapped his leg and sent him sprawling on the stage. The scene of gaiety changed to one of panic, and the curtain flew down to hide it from the horrified audience.

"Justin! *Justin!*" His castmates were shouting in horror, and so was the director and his sister. When had Janelle decided to come to the performance?

A hand on his shoulder yanked him out of the scene. He wasn't onstage, but in his sister's apartment and the throes of the same nightmare that came with renewed horror every time. "What?"

"I could ask the same of you!" Janelle stood at the side of his bed wearing a pink nightshirt and a shocked expression. "I could hear you moaning from across the hall, and you were thrashing like crazy when I came in."

Now that he was awake, he wondered how he'd missed how twisted the sheets had become, not to mention how much he'd soaked them in sweat. He hadn't had a flashback to the accident in weeks, but it was back in full force. "Bad dream. Sorry. Go back to bed."

"No, I'm awake and I have to be at Grand Central for 8:30 anyway." She sighed. "I think I'll make some coffee. Come with me if you want any."

"Thanks." He put on a t-shirt over the sweats he slept in and met his sister in the kitchen. His alarm wasn't supposed to go off for another hour or two, but he didn't want to go back to sleep if this was what was waiting for him.

As the coffee brewed, Janelle took two mugs out of the cabinet. "You know, I'm going to be at the wedding all weekend. If you want to invite Charlie over for a night while I'm away, I don't mind."

Justin sighed. "Thanks, but that's not going to be an issue anymore. It's over."

She paused at the counter. "What? When did this happen?"

"A few days ago."

"More to the point, how did this happen?"

He sighed. "It turns out I'm doing my internship with the architect who's designing the condo that will go up after their building's razed."

Janelle slowly exhaled as she leaned against the counter. "Oh, that is … unfortunate."

"Yeah. They found out, they didn't take it well, I got mad at them for blowing up at me like that—"

understatements of the century, "and we haven't talked since."

She busied herself pouring coffee for a moment before handing Justin a mug. "That's terrible. You seemed so happy this summer, and I know how much they care about you."

"Cared," he corrected.

Janelle frowned, but didn't speak right away. "Suddenly it doesn't seem like a coincidence that I haven't seen them at work since Monday. This is the first time I've ever seen them take a sick day, now that I think about it."

"So?" He tried to sound nonchalant, but concern flared up in spite of himself. Why should he care what happened to Charlie after all the things they'd said?

"So they don't take time off for no reason. I should've known something was wrong, and hearing this tells me they're as torn up about it as you are. I never imagined this, for either of you." She looked down somberly as she stirred light cream into her coffee.

"It couldn't have been anything anyway, not when I'm going back to school in a few weeks." He told her the same thing he'd been telling himself.

"You go to school in New Jersey, not New Delhi," she reminded him. "And even if you did, I never imagined anything, even distance, could break apart what you two were starting. You two were so good together, and I'm really sorry."

"Thanks." He hugged his sister good-bye as she left for the train station a short while later, and then got ready for work.

When he got to the office, he didn't even stop at his desk before he knocked on his boss's door. The great Bernardo Herrera had been out of the office for the past two days, but a crack of light and smell of espresso indicated that he was back.

"Yes?" the voice boomed out.

"It's Justin, and I have some questions about the Lower East Side project."

Bernardo Herrera opened the door a crack. "Then I encourage you to direct them to Denise or Conor. I have received another commission, am in the middle of a design, and do not wish to be interrupted at this time."

"I would, but I don't know if they can answer them. I know what the Lower East Side project is going to look like, I know how you got the idea for it, I know the basic timetable, but I don't know what's going to happen to everyone there now."

His boss frowned. "Two of the buildings have been abandoned for years. That's one reason the development team was able to get them so cheap. They've been falling apart, and everyone on the community board agrees that it will be good to see something new and beautiful rise in their place."

"Great. But what about the other two buildings? People still live there, and where are they going to go? Can they live in the new place, or—"

Bernardo Herrera frowned and handed him a business card. "You are asking questions only the developer can answer, and I suggest you reach out to him. I have said it before and I will say it again: once the last of the holdouts have moved out of the occupied buildings, we can start—"

"They're people, not holdouts." He would never have dared interrupt his boss in the early days of the internship, but things had changed too much since then.

"Justin, I will remind you that we are an architecture firm, not a housing charity. And while you are at my architecture firm, I advise you to get to work. I need your help to carry out my vision of the future, not worry about relics of the past."

Bernardo Herrera firmly closed his office door, and Justin headed back to his desk, seething all the while. He'd spent the past few months toying with the possibility of becoming an architect, but he didn't want to go into the business of throwing people out of the only homes some of them had ever known just so he could build a tribute to himself. He wished he could talk to Charlie about this as he had everything else that had ever bothered him.

In that moment, he missed conversations with them as much as he missed having them in his arms. There were lots of architecture firms in the city, never mind the whole country, but only one person who'd made him feel this way. That in turn reminded him of the morning's conversation with Janelle and how she'd seen more than he thought. Regret turned his stomach all the way over and sent him barreling into the men's room.

He couldn't say how much time he'd spent bent over the toilet before a pounding on the stall door startled him. "Hey, you okay?" someone asked in alarm.

Justin grunted out a reply to send the guy on his way, but he wasn't okay. He didn't see how he could get anything done in this condition, but he didn't want to get on the subway like this. Either way, he couldn't stay here all day. He hefted himself off the bathroom floor, trying to ignore the tilt of the room as he headed to the sink.

He opened the door to find Conor standing there looking askance. "If you're that sick, you're not doing anyone any favors by staying. Take a cab home and come back on Monday if you're better then."

He held out a twenty from a distance. Justin took it and left the office with a swimming head and an aching heart. He hailed a cab with the realization that he hadn't been this sick since he'd come out of anesthesia from the surgery that had helped him heal, but hadn't been enough to let him dance again. Seeing as that was the last time he'd lost something he loved, it was all too fitting.

The thought of the word *love* was a fist of regret that clenched his stomach. The cabbie looked at him in concern as he moaned and heaved, but there was nothing left. There didn't seem to be anything left at all in his life, come to think of it.

Chapter Twenty-Two

"Charlie?"

Charlie looked up from their work at their desk. In the time that had passed since their fight with Justin, they'd been stepping away from actually tending the bar and spending more time in the office. The administrative work bored the hell out of them, but it was better than spending the day with a knot in their stomach that shrank their already small appetite to nonexistent.

"There's someone at the bar to see you," Janelle said. At the look on their face, she sighed and added, "It's not Justin, if that's what you're worried about. He doesn't even come here anymore. All he does is mope around my place after work, so you can go back to the bar whenever you want."

They couldn't decide whether to be relieved, concerned, or disappointed. "Then who is it?"

"Her name's Barb. She's a little older than I am, and she's wearing a gray dress."

It took a moment for it to register who this even was, but then they remembered. "Oh. Great. I'll be down soon."

"I'll tell her on the way out." She picked up a tote bag from beneath her desk and headed to the door.

"Where are you headed?"

"I just joined a gym near my place, and I have a fitness evaluation tonight."

"Cool. Have fun."

After she left, Charlie headed downstairs. The bar seemed to be running smoothly in their absence, but still looked a little less crowded than they would have liked to see. Janelle's description helped them find the well-groomed broker. "Are you Barb?"

She smiled professionally. "And you must be

Charlie. I heard you're moving."

"Yeah." To put off the conversation and to pull themself together, they asked, "Before we start, can I get you anything?"

"Just a club soda, please."

They frowned. "That's all?"

Her expression matched theirs. "I'd normally ask for a Chardonnay, but I'm on a summer allergy medication that doesn't mix well with alcohol."

Charlie reached for a glass, but not the club soda tap. Not right away. Maybe she couldn't have the wine itself, but they could certainly make her something that was every bit as crisp and refreshing. Definitely some citrus … they mostly used the melon balls in the fridge to garnish the punch, but those might work here…

"Try this," they said, handing her the glass. "There's no alcohol in it, but it should still be refreshing."

Barb took a tentative sip that lit up her face. "This is incredible!"

Her compliment improved their mood slightly and made them wonder if there was a market for the virgin cocktails they made for themself so they could join in the fun without undoing their recovery. Barb couldn't possibly be the only one in the city who couldn't drink for medical reasons, and Justin had liked their nonalcoholic drinks, too. The very thought of him crushed their tentatively lifted spirits.

"…prompted your departure?" Barb's voice broke into their thoughts.

"Sorry. What?"

She smiled patiently. "I was asking what made you decide to move."

"I don't have much of a choice in the matter. My building got sold to a developer, and they're putting up a condo in its place."

"And the Lower East Side is one of the most in-demand New York neighborhoods right now," Barb finished, confirming what they were getting thoroughly sick of hearing these days.

"I know. I never would've been able to get in if I'd moved here now."

"When did you move here?" she asked.

"I moved to New York ... wow, eleven years ago."

"And how much are you paying in rent?"

They told her the figure, and she inhaled. "You know, there are some places where you'd be paying less every month on a mortgage and maintenance. You could potentially be looking to buy."

"Except that I don't have enough to make a down payment. I had to eat into my savings when we were getting started here. I've been working on building that back up, but it's not enough."

"So do you want to rent again?" she asked.

"I don't know. If it's true that I could spend less and actually own a place, that makes more sense. But if I can't even get off the ground..." Their voice trailed off.

Barb took another sip of her drink. "Then let me know when you decide what you want to do."

The woman was far too professional to come out and say that they'd wasted her time, but Charlie could see that they had. While they didn't know what to do about their living situation, they knew they would have preferred to have been up in the office and not being told what a failure they were.

Suddenly they missed Justin again and wished they could talk to him about this. He knew what it was like to make choices that turned out to be the wrong ones, and he also knew how to pick himself up from that and move forward with his life. Heaven knew they could use some of that, both in the wake of losing their home and the hottest, most resilient guy they'd ever been with.

****

A text buzzed on his phone, and Justin lifted himself off the couch to check it. Janelle again, asking, **You coming in tonight?**

No thanks. The past few weeks had shown him that he'd gotten spoiled eating all those amazing meals for the first half of the summer, but he didn't want to go back until he'd figured out how to make things right with Charlie, or at least less awkward. Because of that, he spent his days going to his internship and then straight to Janelle's apartment every night, where he was slowly eating his way through a collection of dusty canned soups and freezer-burnt Trader Joe's meals for dinner most nights. He couldn't bring himself to face anyone else, even the person delivering a Seamless order.

They're not at the bar, if that's what you're worried about.

I'm not, I'm just tired. The tired part was true, but the part about not being worried about seeing them was a lie. He wanted to, but didn't know how he could do that and keep his internship.

It took a moment or two for the next message to come in. **Then see you later. I'll bring something back for you.**

Thanks. He put his phone in the charger, then turned his attention back to the TV. Reruns of legal procedurals had been one of a few things to distract him from his ballooning stomach while he'd waited for his cast to come off, and it was still something he returned to in bored or depressed moments.

A raised voice on the screen snapped him out of his stupor. Characters argued until one of the detectives admitted that his family had a sordid history with the executive the team was investigating. The chief took him off the case, citing the conflict of interest, but it looked like he'd still have his job.

As the show cut to commercial, it occurred to Justin that maybe that was the answer. Maybe if he worked on anything but the Lower East Side project for the rest of his internship, he'd be able to keep it, clear his conscience, and make things right with Charlie. He turned off the TV, spent the evening in a more cheerful mood after Janelle returned with dinner, and slept peacefully for the first time since the fight.

"Morning, Denise," he said as he took his seat the next morning.

"Morning, Justin." She looked up from her computer. "You look like you're in a better mood. Did you hear Mr. Herrera wants you to take a trip with him to the Lower East Side project site today?"

He sighed. "I can't do that."

Denise frowned. "Of course you can. You've been doing great for weeks. You can handle this, and aren't you the one who said you wanted to more actual architecture work? This is your chance."

"And as great as that sounds, I can't take it. I have a conflict with that project."

Denise typed something, then looked back up at him. "Mr. Herrera wants to see you in his office."

Justin had a pretty good idea what this was about, but wasn't looking forward to talking to his ultimate boss all the same. He stood, straightened his spine, and headed to the corner office.

"Close the door and sit down." Once he had obeyed the orders, Bernardo Herrera asked, "Now what is this Denise is saying about you refusing to do your work today?"

"That's not what I meant. I'm perfectly willing do work. It's just that the Lower East Side project is going to be a problem. I was dating someone who lives in one of those buildings, and I can't work on this and be objective about it."

"Again, you seem confused about where you work. Do you think people get to make calls like that in this business? Do you think this is a democracy? You are wrong on both counts, and I have more important things to do than babysit the interns."

"And I'm not asking you to. I'm just asking that I get taken off this particular project, to work on any and every project *but* this one. Otherwise I don't know if I can continue here." He didn't know if he was in a position to make threats like that, but he did know every word he said was true.

His boss's frown deepened. "It's lucky for you that it's far too late in the summer to hire someone else, or your next and last task would be to clean out your desk. If you can't or won't do anything on the Lower East Side project, you will spend the rest of your summer in the administrative work that helps this firm run smoothly. Do you understand?"

"Yes, sir."

"And you're going down this path anyway?"

He stood firm. "Yes, sir."

Justin returned to his desk and got to work on the proofreading Bernardo had sent him out with. He hadn't been looking forward to returning to college, but staying in New York with this internship and without Charlie wasn't an appealing prospect, either.

Chapter Twenty-Three

Charlie collapsed on their bed. They hadn't had to go to work today, but the apartment hunt was turning into a second full-time gig. Barb the broker understood that the restaurant kept them too busy to go to open houses on weekends, so she arranged appointments at listings throughout the week and on their days off with the result that they couldn't remember the last time they'd had a day that was completely their own.

They wouldn't have objected if they thought they were getting anywhere, literally and figuratively, but all they were learning was what they didn't want. They'd never fancied themself a material person, but they had no idea how they could fit their stuff into some of these Manhattan places. There were bigger apartments to be found in the outer boroughs, but no scene, community, or even bodegas around. And the one time they found something they would have considered, the landlord had answered their question about pets with, "Hell, no." Well, that was exactly what they said to that particular listing.

Most annoyingly, they found themself wishing they could run their dilemma by Justin. As someone who knew what it was like to lose everything, he'd help them feel less alone and see that it was possible to start over. And if he couldn't solve their problems, he could at least touch or kiss them in a way that made them forget everything if only for the moment.

They reminded themself for the millionth time that he was working for the enemy, but it couldn't drive out the memories of the dates, conversations, and orgasms the two of them had shared. If anything, all the good memories were threatening to crowd out the bad ones and make them feel worse about how things had gone down those weeks ago. The more the confrontation replayed in their head, the more ridiculous and unhinged they knew they sounded, and the more justified he'd be in refusing to see them ever again.

As they lay there ruminating, Charlie noticed that they'd placed their hands over their heart. It brought on a happier memory, and they ran their hands over their chest and stomach in the same way he had on that particularly magic night. They didn't feel anything except silly. What had he done differently that sent shivers of ecstasy through their entire body? They didn't know, and they didn't even feel like turning over to touch themself so as to release tension. It was as if all the pleasure receptors in their body had shut down.

Their phone rang, and they glanced at the screen. They hesitated about picking it up, wondering if they could take the sound of the name they hated for however long she wanted to ramble. At the same time, they would have welcomed contact from anyone. "Hi, Mom."

"Hi, Elsie."

They winced. "How's everything going there?"

Molly rabbited on for a while about events at home and people they didn't know anymore, if at all. They made approving noises and asked questions, but she wasn't fooled. "Are you okay? You don't sound so good."

There was no use trying to pretend otherwise. "It's been a rough week. Rough couple of weeks, really."

"What's wrong?" She sounded truly sympathetic.

"I'm having trouble finding a new place," they began, "and things went south with the guy I've been seeing."

"What happened? Did you tell him about your … sex thing?"

Charlie bristled. "If you're talking about my

gender identity, why would you automatically jump to that as the reason any relationship of mine goes wrong?"

"Because that's … well, it's a lot to lay on someone. I know how confusing and difficult it was for me when you explained."

That was evident in the fact that she still insisted on calling them the name they were supposed to have left in the middle of nowhere. "He didn't think it was. He didn't just accept me for who I am, he embraced me."

The realization sent a knife through their heart, and their mom's vexed squeak didn't help. "Well, I'm glad to hear that, but I don't see why you're snapping at me, Elsie."

"Because you're my mother, and you're supposed to support me instead of assuming the worst about me just because I'm gender-fluid, something you don't understand and never made any attempt to! What would you say if you found out this ended on a day I was wearing a dress as pretty as any you ever tried to force me into?" The dress in question was buried at the bottom of the laundry basket, and it wasn't looking likely that they'd wear it again after that night.

"What would you say if I said he was a liar and a betrayer—would you even think of that? Or would that still be my fault for being who I am?" Charlie ended the call and turned off their phone, pacing around the apartment to burn off the excess energy that had suddenly sprung up.

It would have been so much easier if that was the whole truth and they could hate Justin and move on with their life. Unfortunately for Charlie, it wasn't as clear-cut as that. Now that some time had passed, they were willing to concede that there was no way he could have known them or that any of this was going to happen when he accepted the internship. At the same time, now that he did know, he was going about it all the wrong way.

Then again, what was the right way? Did they want him to quit his internship? No way, not if that would put a black mark on his record and send him away from New York for good. But they didn't want to hear about what a brilliant architect his boss was, all the fun he was having in the internship, and how he was going to make a future for himself putting up a glass monstrosity where their home used to be.

Memories of the fight and Justin's hurt expression resurfaced to fill them with shame and stop them in their tracks. Of course it had been a shock to find out where he was working, but suddenly that no longer felt like an excuse for flying off the handle … or a good enough reason to push away one of the most amazing people they'd ever met.

Charlie picked up the phone again. They wanted to talk to him and apologize, but remembered that they couldn't blame him if he never wanted to talk to them again after their wild accusations. The thought hit them like a punch to the gut, and they put the phone down.

Suddenly, the walls of their home seemed to close in and make the apartment too small to contain them. They checked on Willow's food and water bowls, grabbed their wallet with the unlimited Metrocard in it, and headed out the door. They didn't know where they were going, but they had to get away from this and forget everything that had gone on in the past few hours.

****

"You sure you don't want to come tonight?" Janelle asked on the phone. "It's Charlie's day off, if that's what you're worried about."

"Thanks, but I don't feel like going out tonight." He hadn't felt like going out any night lately.

Janelle sighed. "Then I'll see you around tennish. I'm doing a yoga class to wind down after I get off here."

Justin cracked a smile. "And you say I don't quit. You're spending a lot of time at the gym lately."

Janelle sighed again. "Look, I love you, and Charlie's great to work with, but lately it seems like there's no escaping what happened between the two of you. You're moping around my place; they're holed up in the office and completely depressed... If neither of you are going to work this out or move on, I need to take a break and spend some time in a place where no one knows what's going on with you two because no one ever met either one of you."

After she hung up, Justin decided that his sister was right and enough was enough. He reached for his phone and pulled up Charlie's number. He called it, but it went straight to voicemail. "Hi! You have reached Charlie Ashton. I don't have my phone on me at the moment, but leave me a message or send a text and we'll be in touch soon."

The same thing happened when he tried calling three more times. As good as it was to hear their voice again to some degree, it was frustrating to keep hearing it say the same thing. Did they have their phone off, or had they blocked his number? Either way, he finally decided to leave a message so he could tell himself he'd tried. "Hey, Charlie, it's Justin. I guess we both needed some time to sort things out, but I was hoping we could catch up and ... I don't know. Just call or text me back."

An hour later, Charlie had done neither. Justin sent a short **Everything ok?** text, but they didn't answer it. Even after that strained first date, or when he'd inadvertently called them at work, they'd still sent a reply that he didn't realize how much he'd come to count on until now. So either they'd blocked him, or there was a worse reason they weren't answering.

He picked up his phone again, but didn't call them. Instead, he ran a search for "Kelsey FDNY" and got a hit before long. He didn't recognize the picture at first—the woman's severe bun and dark clothes were the polar opposite of what he'd seen at the barbecue—but a closer look showed a familiar face and how to find her.

"What's your emergency?" the operator asked.

"Can I talk to Kelsey Matthews?"

Instead of being patched through, the operator let out the verbal equivalent of an eyeroll. "This is seriously why you called the fire department?"

He sighed. "I need to talk to her, and I don't have her cell number."

"Well, she's not here. Her truck went out on a call about twenty minutes ago and they're still at the scene." The operator sounded around his own age and thoroughly exasperated. "Can I take a message?"

"Please. Tell her Justin Robbins called, and that it's about Charlie." He gave his number, thanked him, and hung up. He didn't know what else to do, but maybe he'd done everything he could at this point.

She didn't call back for another hour and a half. "Is this Justin?"

"Yes. Hi. How'd it go?"

"No one on my team was hurt, and the victim's going to be fine," she said warily, "but you didn't call to ask about that, did you?"

"Uh, no."

"So what's going on? Cal said it was about Charlie."

"Yeah." He took a deep breath. "I guess they're not with you if you're at work now, but how are they?"

She answered his question with one of her own. "Why are you asking me?"

"Because we haven't spoken in weeks, and now they're not even answering their phone. I'd understand if they were at work, but it's their day off. I was worried and thought you'd at least know what's going on with them."

Kelsey's tone of annoyance gave way to one of concern. "I don't know because I haven't seen them in weeks, either. Not since just after the Fourth."

"Then can you try calling them? I understand if they're avoiding me, but maybe they'll talk to you."

"Sure. Give me a sec."

She hung up and called him back sooner than he would have liked. "They're not picking up for me, either. Sorry I can't be more helpful."

"There's nothing else you can do?"

"I'm a firefighter, not a cop," she reminded him, "and I don't think there's anything anyone can do until they decide they're ready to talk."

"But what if…" He let his voice trail off rather than let out the worried thoughts that had swirled ever since she'd called back without news.

"If anything's happened, my team will be the first on the scene," she said in a firm but reassuring tone he remembered from the EMTs who'd taken him to the hospital after his accident. "And if I hear from them, I'll keep you posted and tell them to call you. How's that?"

"Fine, thanks. Thanks for everything." What else could he say?

She hung up, and he slumped back on the couch. He'd hoped calling Kelsey would make things better, but he only felt worse. If anything had happened to them before he could make things right again, no job or internship would be worth it.

Chapter Twenty-Four

Charlie stood across the street from an unknown bar in an unknown neighborhood. They hadn't really thought about where they were going, just gotten on the subway, picked a stop once the train had started to run aboveground, and then walked a few streets.

It had taken a lot of work just to find this place. Barb had told them it'd be smart to buy in this part of Brooklyn. It was apparently on the up and up, but they weren't seeing much to indicate that this was the case. Some of these streets were more populated with warehouses than the residential buildings they were used to seeing in Manhattan, and it looked about as quiet as Kansas. But they'd finally found a main street and passed a few blocks of chain restaurants and stores before finding this hole in the wall. If it had taken all this work for them to get here, it wasn't likely anyone they knew would find them here, either. That thought pushed them through the door and into a stool on the end, away from the small crowd gathered in the center.

"What can I get you?" the grizzled bartender asked as he noticed them.

"Rum and Coke, and make it a double. Please." It came out before they could stop themself. That had been their cocktail of choice when they were trying to get through college and feel even a little more comfortable in their own skin. Now, though, they couldn't remember the last time they'd had one.

He poured two shots of rum into a glass, topped it off with soda from the tap, and handed it to Charlie. They made a face at the sip they took. They could mix up a rum and Coke in their sleep, and they would not have paired this particular variety with that soda. Of course it was supposed to be a sweet drink, but this version was sickeningly so.

Then again, they weren't here for a tasting. They were here to forget the condo conversion, the fight … even their own name if they were lucky. They picked up the glass, tilted their head back, and drained as much of the glass as they could without tasting it.

As they put the glass back down on the bar, tears sprang to their eyes as they coughed and spluttered. This drink didn't just taste like shit; it also tasted like failure. They'd come so far, worked so hard, and now they were throwing it away on one revolting cocktail. Kelsey wouldn't be pleased to hear about this—they knew they were supposed to call her if they felt like doing this, but they'd only been thinking about escaping.

And then there was everything Justin had said about how brave they were to work in the face of what they were trying to avoid every day. The thought of his praise and him on the whole sent their head into their hands and piled sorrow on top of the shame.

They'd managed to stop coughing, but the tears kept coming and Charlie didn't even try to keep them at bay. They'd gone out in the hopes of seeking oblivion, but all this terrible drink had brought was an uncomfortable awareness of everything they'd lost. Every bottle behind the bar wouldn't be enough to make them forget, and the realization made them cry harder. To make matters worse, their nose was getting too stuffed to breathe.

As they sat doubled over sobbing on the stool, the bartender peered at them. "You okay there, uh…"

"Fine," they snapped before they had to watch him debate whether to call them sir or ma'am. "I just better close this out."

Charlie shoved the nearly empty glass away, blew their nose into a cocktail napkin, and held another one to their eyes. Once they felt themself calming down, they put some bills on the bar and walked out only to realize they had no idea where they were. They reached in their pocket to get out their phone and pull up a map only to grasp nothing but lip balm. Sighing, they turned around and headed back in.

"Back so soon?" the geezer at the bar asked.

"I'm not ordering. I just need my phone back," they said curtly.

He frowned. "Then it's wherever you left it, pal. No one turned anything in, and I didn't see you with a phone anyway. I know because you're the first person I've seen without one in weeks."

Had they really walked out phoneless? How did that even happen in this day and age? Charlie didn't say any of this, just thanked him and left. They'd gotten completely turned around, and it took longer than it should have to find the main street. Once there, the subway wasn't exactly making itself known. This neighborhood wasn't menacing, just confusing and impossible to find transportation in without a guide. How and why had they forgotten something so important?

Just as they started to concede that they'd have to find a bridge and walk back to Manhattan, a cab came and they hailed it. There were days when they thought taking the subway to Helga's from their part of the Lower East Side was annoying, but that was a walk in the park compared to this nonsense. They couldn't live here, and made a mental note to tell Barb that the next time she sent them listings to think about.

Charlie didn't live that far into Manhattan, but the price of the cab ride stunned them out of their stupor. Back upstairs, the first thing they saw was Willow looking at them accusingly, followed closely by their phone on the kitchen counter. They sighed, stroked her head, and headed into the bathroom to purge the drink.

A short time later, they stood up shakily, sprayed air freshener around the bathroom, and brushed their teeth. They knew out of body, out of mind wasn't how this worked, but they just wanted all traces of that thing gone.

A few swishes of Listerine burned their throat but thoroughly obliterated any last tastes that might have tried to linger in their mouth. That calmed them down enough to power their phone on, only to be floored by the number of notifications and voicemails. They went out for a few hours and what happened?

To their great shock, Justin's number came up the most among the missed calls, and he'd left a message. The rumble over the phone line calmed their nerves in a way that swill at the bar was supposed to, and they barely even registered his words at first.

They replayed the message to listen to what he was actually saying, and it sent them into a state of confusion. They still didn't know what either one could say or do that would make things better, just like they didn't know what would happen if they saw him again.

To buy some time as they decided what to do, Charlie turned their attention to the rest of the messages. Inevitably, their mother had left a message. They were in no rush to hear about what an undesirable child they were, so they skipped that and looked back at the list of missed calls.

One was from Marcus, the bartender on duty that night. "Hey, Charlie, if you make up new recipes, you ought to share them with the rest of us. Someone came in asking for the specialty cocktail you made her friend, said it didn't have any alcohol in it, and I didn't know what she was talking about."

Charlie immediately knew what he was talking

about, but couldn't remember the last time they'd made those drinks for anyone except Justin … and Barb the broker. How many people had she told about this? They didn't know, but the idea soothed their ego and inspired them to text him back: **Sorry. Once I'm back and see what I have to work with, I'll write it down for everyone.**

After they sent the reply, they turned back to the list and saw a text from Kelsey: **Are you okay?**

Guilt about making her worry piled onto the shame of the night, and they touched the message to reply. But before they could, they saw another message in her queue with a time stamp of an hour earlier: **If you don't want to talk to your guy, just tell him. He can't call the firehouse about things like this.**

Their eyes widened as they replied, **What are you talking about?**

Welcome back. Before they could respond to that, she sent a follow-up saying, **When you didn't answer your phone, Justin called my house looking for you. What's going on?**

Tell you at the meeting tomorrow—heaven knew Charlie would have plenty to talk about then—**but I'm fine now. Sorry to go dark**.

Don't be sorry. Call him back so he doesn't pull another stunt like this.

First the voicemail, now this… It was starting to feel like they didn't have any choice but to get back in touch with him. The thought elated them more than they would have liked.

****

Justin toyed with an overheated quiche as he waited at an unfamiliar café chain near his office. It was such a relief to be away from there after a morning of cleaning the conference room and sorting a newly printed archive of press clippings by date. Bernardo Herrera seemed determined to call his bluff, and had evidently told Conor and Denise not to give him anything too interesting to do. This wasn't an internship anymore. It was a battle of wills, and he was determined to win it. Only a few more days of sticking it out.

For the millionth time since he'd last seen them, he wondered what Charlie would say about this. He thought back to other conversations he'd had with them, and he couldn't remember them inserting themself into things when he'd had a problem. They'd always heard him out before asking questions that would lead him to the right conclusions. It was a shame that having their building in the mix would color their opinion on this.

As it occurred to him that Charlie should be here any minute, they walked in and found him at the table. They looked as put-together as ever, but a little rougher somehow. A closer look showed dark circles that their concealer couldn't totally hide, and their glow had faded. "Hey."

"Hey. Did you get anything?"

"My latte should be ready soon." They glanced around. "It's so weird to be out in the middle of the work day. I'd usually be eating something Lena made me in the back of the restaurant."

"I know what you mean. I've been eating in an office cafeteria all summer."

"Ah, yes." Their spine stiffened a bit at that. "How's that going?"

He frowned. "Would it make you feel better if I said I think the new design's hideous? After all the time I've spent in your neighborhood and seen what else is around your building, I can see that this is going to look as ridiculous as if someone started twerking in the middle of *Swan Lake*."

Charlie cracked a smile. "I might actually pay to see that."

"Because it'd be a freak show, just like this thing's going to be." Just like everything Bernardo Herrera designed, now that he really thought about it. It was becoming clear that these buildings got attention and ink for being the opposite of their surroundings. Sometimes it worked, but sometimes it just plain did not.

"Then how are you still working there?"

"It's almost over, and—"

A barista called Charlie's name before he could finish, and they rose from their seat, saying, "Tell me when I get back."

They headed to the counter, giving Justin a few seconds to gather his thoughts. He only had an hour for lunch, and he didn't want to waste it talking about work or on the smallest of talk. It had been such a relief when they'd gotten back in touch and agreed to see him, and he wanted to make sure they knew that.

Charlie couldn't have been away for more than a full minute, but they came back to the table with their face carefully controlled and their posture rigid. As they stirred a packet of sugar into their steaming mug, they gave him only the briefest glance up. "Sorry about that. What were you going to say?"

"That I'm sorry for everything," he said. "I didn't want any of this. I didn't want to hurt you. I really regret that I did, and I don't want to go back to school with this unresolved. I also don't want you to think any of the time I spent with you was a conspiracy to get you out of your building, because it wasn't."

Their expression of nonchalance turned to one of embarrassment. "I don't know if I really thought that, and I shouldn't have blown up at you like that. I was just so…"

They paused, and their expression had now turned to one of anguish. Justin didn't say anything, just let them talk. "I've been so scared about this all summer—wondering where I'm going to live next, having my home taken away from me, worrying about how I'm going to pack up my whole life... I can't go down to the developer's office and yell at them for ruining my life, so I let it all out on you when I found out about your connection to the project—*not* that that's any excuse for anything I said or did. You didn't design this thing, you didn't decide where to put it, and it was really wrong of me to take it out on you. *I'm* the one who's sorry, and I can't say it enough."

The more they spoke, the more he softened towards them. "You didn't do it on purpose. Neither of us did. It was all a bunch of accidents, you living where you do, me working where I do, me meeting you and then feeling the way I do."

Finally, something seemed to break through their armor. "Do, not did?" they asked.

"Do," he admitted. "None of it changed what we did together or how happy I was through all of it."

"And none of it changed for me, either. It would've been so much easier if it had, but I still thought about you, still wanted you..."

"I still want you, too, but it was never just a sex thing to me."

"So what was—*is* it? One of those backstage hookups like you told me about?"

"If only for the limited time, and it's running out," he had to admit.

"I know. You said this is almost over. You'll be back at school soon, and I'm meeting you now because my life outside work's been completely taken over by the apartment hunt."

"How's that going, anyway?" Before they could answer, he added, "I'm not asking for my boss. I'm asking for me because I want to know what's going on with you."

Charlie sighed. "Not great. Between the buyout offer I got and my savings, it won't go far enough to let me find anything I like in a neighborhood I could stand to live in. I don't know where that leaves me."

"I'm sorry to hear that." He tentatively reached his hand across the table. "But most of all, I'm glad I met you but sorry it happened when it did. If I'd found you sooner and known what was happening, I never would have taken this internship."

Charlie didn't move. "But if you hadn't taken it, how would I ever have met you?"

"I don't know. I could've gone to visit my sister at the restaurant where she works and met an especially cute bartender. I mean, I go to college in New Jersey, not New Delhi," he said, echoing Janelle's words from that morning.

They smiled sadly. "And what would've prompted that? She'd been working here for a few months by the time you came, so why now?"

"I don't know." He sighed. "I don't know what else to say except thank you. This was one of the best summers of my life, and all because of you."

Charlie's face softened. "This condo conversion made it a scary summer for me, but you made me forget all about it. I was always so happy with you, and…"

Their voice trailed off as they extended their hand across the table to meet his, and he took it. Time was running out on his break, but he didn't want to go back to the office or do anything but stay in this moment.

Charlie slowly pulled away. "I have to get back to work."

"Yeah, it's time for me to go, too."

They gathered their bag, and he straightened the back of his shirt after rising from his chair. Then his eyes met theirs, and he couldn't have said who wrapped whose arms around the other first. They fit way too easily, and he closed his eyes to seal in the memory of their touch and scent.

He lowered his head so his lips touched the top of their head, and whispered, "I'll never forget you."

"Neither will I." Their voice reverberated throughout his body, and he held them closer, stroking the back of their head and moving all the way down their back. Charlie didn't move, just held him tight and didn't let go. He didn't want them to.

Chapter Twenty-Five

For the millionth time, Charlie reflected that this whole summer would be so much easier if Justin had been even a tiny bit in the wrong. Then they could walk away from him feeling light and free, not like their body had been put through a meat grinder. Rather like they felt now, come to think of it, despite knowing this day was coming even at the height of their happiness with him. They held their posture rigid and set their face so they could walk away without collapsing in grief.

The memory of his smile and his hands on their body cheered them for a moment, but then the memory of what they'd lost crowded in and brought tears to their eyes. They couldn't take another breakdown like the one at the dive bar, so they stepped aside, squeezing their eyes shut until the feeling passed. Despite being able to see clearly again when they opened their eyes, they didn't feel any better.

But they couldn't afford the luxury of taking another sick day and going home to wallow as they had after the fight. They had a bar to run, and too many people at the restaurant that needed them. They squared their shoulders, opened the door, and headed back to the bar.

Mila looked up with a frazzled expression. "Charlie! Thank goodness you're back."

They stirred in concern. "What's wrong?"

"Well, it's not quite wrong, but… Good news, just about everyone at that lunch meeting wanted one of your mocktails. Bad news, we ran out of melon balls because of it, and I don't know what to give them instead."

Charlie's spirits significantly lifted at that. "Oops. Let me see what else we have to work with and I'll figure something out. Once I do, you can watch me mix and learn the recipe that way."

They peeked in the kitchen. "Chef? Lena?"

She looked up from the stove. "What's up?"

"Anything good at the greenmarket?"

She looked thoughtful as she stirred. "I didn't make it there today, but cherries are back in season. I'll get you some."

A kitchen assistant handed Charlie a bowl of fruit—cherries, blueberries, blackberries, raspberries—and they took it back to the bar with their mind working. A lot of red wines had cherry and berry notes, after all ... there was no reason this had to be sweet, that's what tonic water was for... They muddled some cherries and berries together with mint leaves. Mila watched them work, and soon another round was ready for the crowd.

Mila got back to serving the other bar patrons, but Charlie kept working with the remainder of the berries. They peeked in the bar's minifridge, poured pomegranate juice over the muddled fruit, and added club soda before taking a sip. They frowned, added a squeeze of lime, and had another taste. Better.

A *lot* better, now that they thought about it. This was delicious, and being creative again had forced their mind off their heartbreak. The thought threatened to resurface, so Charlie took another, larger sip and forced themself to think about what they should be doing with these cocktails in the future.

As they enjoyed their drink, the group filed out of the restaurant. One of the men paused at the bar. "Who made the mocktails?" he asked.

Mila gestured to them. "We both handled the actual mixing, but Charlie came up with the recipe."

He gave them an appraising look. "I don't know if you knew, but we're the editorial staff of *New York*

Scene and here on a lunch meeting. I've covered the food before, but don't remember coming across anyone anywhere who's put this much thought into nonalcoholic drinks. I have to get back to work now, but can we sit down and talk about this some more later?"

Charlie beamed. "Of course!"

The two of them set up a time for him to come back, and Charlie watched him go with a smile spreading across their face and a glow of excitement expanding through their chest. Ever since Helga's had opened, diners had raved about how Lena made things they couldn't find anywhere else. Maybe now it was their turn to put the bar on the map and get their name in the food columns and blogs.

As a matter of fact, maybe it was turning out to be a good thing that they and Justin had left things the way they did. All questions of what was going to happen next were answered, after all. And without this cluttering up their brain, they'd be freer to create and go forward with their life and bar.

If only they actually believed that. The imaginary accolades would only be a hollow victory without anyone to share it with. Of course Lena would be happy for them, and so would Kelsey, but who else was there? Their mom wouldn't be happy until they were living her idea of a perfect life—one that involved giving up their share in the restaurant, popping out kids, and not thinking about anything else—Willow would probably react to the news by grooming her tail, and the door had closed on telling Justin.

As they trudged up to the office, they took out their phone again and saw yet another notification, one of a missed call and voicemail from an unfamiliar 212 number. They pressed "play".

"Hi, Charlie, I'm calling on behalf of Kenmare

Street Development. We sent you an offer a few weeks ago, but we've heard from your lawyer about your situation and your long-time tenancy. Because of that, we would like to talk to you a little more about this and see what kind of arrangement we can come to. Call us back to arrange an appointment at your convenience."

Their heart flew to their throat at a speed that erased all other emotions. They'd heard horror stories about people who'd taken too long to deal with building conversions and had the electricity and water turned off to drive them out of the building. But in all those scenarios, the outages had come on suddenly. Surely the company wouldn't call to effectively issue a ransom note, would it? There was only one way to find out.

****

Throughout his ballet career, Justin's least favorite part of exams and auditions had been waiting and wondering what would happen next. Even if he didn't get the results he wanted, at least seeing the lists would let him work harder toward his goals without doubts eating away at his focus.

He tried to convince himself that waiting had been the worst part of today, too, but that wasn't true. Not after how he and Charlie had left things. He didn't want to leave things with them at all, but circumstances dictated that there wasn't a choice. He'd known that going in, but that didn't make it hurt any less.

It was not lost on him that almost every tragedy he'd danced ended with someone dying of a broken heart. If he was still in the company, he could channel this pain into extra training, lean on it to inform his storytelling, and possibly see something good come out of it if a critic praised the emotion in his performance. The internship offered no such outlet, but he still trudged to the elevator.

AN ESPECIALLY HOT SUMMER

Denise looked up as he returned. "I see Mr. Sunshine's back," she said with a roll of her eyes.

Justin forced a smile that probably looked more like indigestion. "I'm fine, just shouldn't have had that quiche."

"Then maybe you ought to call it a day." Her frown deepened. "Maybe you ought to call it a day on this internship altogether. It's almost over anyway, so I see no harm in letting you go a few days early. Don't worry, I won't put it on your record."

Her pronouncement stirred him from his stupor. "Did I do something wrong?"

"It's what you *aren't* doing. There isn't enough work for both of us with you on these administrative projects, and I'm the one with the master's degree in architecture and full-time job at the firm. The one who's still waiting to do more than grunt work, and all because Mr. Herrera thinks I'll be quitting to have kids any day now." Her eyes narrowed before he could ask about this. "You're the one who reminds him of himself when he was younger. The one who had a great opportunity and threw it away, so turn in your security pass and don't talk to me, don't look to me for a recommendation."

Justin took out his card, but ignored the last order. It rankled too much for him to let go of easily. "Hey, I told him there was a conflict with the Lower East Side project, and he decided to punish me instead of working around it. And what does it tell you about a guy who'd rather work with an intern than a qualified professional?"

She sighed. "I don't know, but I'm sorry this summer was such a waste of time for you."

"It wasn't. You told me the point of the internship was to see if I wanted to work at a firm like this, and I got an answer to that. Shame it wasn't the one everyone would have liked to hear."

He gathered the few items scattered on his desk and left the office for the last time. His fury carried him through the subway ride and the walk to Janelle's apartment, where he found her sitting on the sofa. "What are you doing here?" he asked.

"My day off," she said, her eyes on the floor.

"Oh yeah."

She glanced up. "More to the point, what are you doing here? Shouldn't you be at your internship?"

"It's over." He took a breath as he realized that was true in too many ways. "It's all over. Charlie and I said good-bye this afternoon."

She didn't look up. "I thought you two were already finished."

"We met up to try to work things out, like you said, and wound up saying good-bye before I left." Every word was another stab through his heart.

She sighed. "Right. I forgot that you have a monopoly on heartbreak, that you're the only one whose life didn't turn out the way he thought it would. Forgive my ignorance, I'll get up to comfort you, I just need a minute now."

Her voice had been rising in volume with every word, and the intensity of her speech gave Justin pause. "Did something happen?"

She sighed and held out a thick card. "This came today."

As he studied the picture of a baby with a blue hat and red, scrunched-up face, he wondered what he was supposed to be seeing. "Not even a month before mine," he said, reading the birthday in swirly blue letters at the top.

Janelle let out an aggravated shriek. "Do you ever think about anyone but yourself? Read the rest!"

"Okay, okay!" He turned back to the card.

"'Nicholas and Anne Lagnate welcomed'… *Oh.*"

As the name dawned on him, he sat down next to her. "Oh, sis, I'm sorry."

She didn't face him. "He said this was what he wanted. He said he'd find someone else who'd do it if I wouldn't, and it's my fault."

He thought back to his sister's divorce and realized he didn't know much about what had happened. "Did you have … problems?"

"He'd say that. We agreed that we'd have five years with just the two of us to travel, get to the top of our careers … do whatever we wanted before starting a family. I'm the one who asked why we couldn't just stay like that and didn't want to remove my implant." Her voice broke, and a tear splashed to the floor.

The sight removed the blinders from Justin's own eyes, and he wrapped his arm around his sister's shoulders as she cried. He knew exactly how she felt, but this wasn't the time to give in to it. It was more important to be there for her.

She reached for a box of tissues on a side table, blotted her eyes, and stood up. "Come on."

"What do you want to do?"

"Freshen up so we can go out for dinner tonight. It's not going to do either of us any good to sit around here moping." She gave him a sidelong look, and her eyes were red but sharp. "I'm also out of Trader Joe's meals."

He mumbled an apology and an offer to buy her more, but knew she was right. His New York world had expanded so much in the time he'd spent with Charlie, but now it had shrunk to smaller than a prison cell. And he wanted to be free.

A few hours later, Justin and Janelle were sitting at a table with sidelong Central Park views in a glass tower. Dinner would be out any minute, but she already looked calmer after a glass of wine and an appetizer. "I'm glad we got out of there. Thanks for coming with me."

"It was my pleasure." He meant it, and promised himself he'd keep in better touch with his sister—texts, calls, maybe a visit or two—once he was back at school. That was something else he could thank Charlie for—would things have ever reached this point if not for his relationship with them?—and the reminder of the closed door smarted.

Chapter Twenty-Six

Charlie paid the cabbie and stepped out on the sidewalk. The developer's office was downtown, but on the complete opposite side of the city from where they lived. A whole string of offices was springing up in the area that used to be totally industrial, now that they looked around. They caught sight of their reflection in a glassy building, and smiled at the sight of their professional outfit, carefully styled hair, and perfect makeup. With any luck, they'd make a good impression and come away with a good deal.

Their ringing phone interrupted their thoughts, and they tensed at the name on the screen. They'd exchanged a few conciliatory emails with their mother since the day of the argument, but they still had reservations about taking this call now. However, if the upcoming meeting demonstrated anything, maybe it was better to get unpleasant things out of the way and off their plate forever.

"Mom? Is everything okay?"

"I'm fine. Are you?" They didn't answer right away, but stayed silent so long that she added, "Elsie? Are you there?"

An all too familiar pain pulsed at their temples. This was the last thing they needed today. "Mom, I know we've been over this. Can you please stop calling me Elsie and start calling me Charlie?"

"But you said I could—"

"Because I thought I could handle it, but it turns out I can't. And if you can't do that, I'm not going to be able to talk right now. I have a meeting coming up, and I can't spend it with a tension headache from hearing a name that's brought me nothing but trouble."

Molly let out a ragged gasp. "Then maybe I won't

be able to talk to you for a while. I shouldn't have to tell you how much it hurts me every time I think about how you rejected your education, your background, and everything your father and I ever gave you."

This was the same guilt trip she'd laid on them that had convinced them to let her call them Elsie, but they refused to give in to it again. "Well, think about this. Once I figured out who I was, I could've called myself anything I wanted—God knows I have my pick of androgynous names—but I still decided to go by Charlie, which I got from my middle name! I didn't reject what you and Dad gave me. I just used it as a foundation to get to who I am now. Isn't that what you were trying to do all along?"

The silence on the other end of the line lasted so long Charlie wondered if the call had been dropped. Molly broke it by saying, "I never thought of it that way."

"Does that help at all?" they asked gently.

"It actually does, a little." Their mom sounded surprised as she hastily added, "Charlie."

"I'm glad," and they meant what they said. They stayed on the call for a few more blocks, and Molly made a point of inserting "Charlie" into every other sentence. Maybe she was hoping they'd get sick of it and tell her to switch back to Elsie, but no such luck. It had taken way too long to hear her call them their real name, and each repetition came as a relief. If this was what it'd take to get her used to it, they'd put up with it into tomorrow morning.

Except that wasn't an option right now. The address had been easier to find than they expected, and they were coming up on it now. "Mom, I'll have to call you later. It's almost time."

"Okay, El—Charlie. Good luck. I love you."

"I love you, too." They hung up the phone with their usual tension headache a shadow of itself already.

Charlie checked in at the front desk and rode the elevator up. Weirdly enough, their nerves about this had faded along with the headache. If they'd managed to get through to their mother, they could handle this.

The receptionist offered them a bottle of water, but they hadn't taken two sips before someone came out to usher them to a conference room overlooking the Hudson River. After the usual "Please, call me Charlie" song and dance, the developer launched into a lecture about how important the project was to the Lower East Side, how it was part of something bigger than just a new luxury condominium… All stuff they already knew, so it was easy to tune out.

"…and you're one of the last ones to respond, which is holding up the project to a certain extent. Why is that?"

The question demanded their attention, and they paused to gather all the thoughts that had piled up since they'd found out about the conversion. Now was their chance to have their say with the one who was really responsible for the project that had utterly destroyed their sense of home and contentment, but they'd lost all desire to rage at the developer. Not to mention everyone they'd talked to—Lena, Janelle, Kelsey, Inez, Barb, the lawyer—had urged them to be calm and polite, as an attitude like that would increase the possibility of a better offer, if there even was one.

Charlie took a deep breath. "It's nothing I was actively trying to do. For one thing, my job running a restaurant is a busy one. For another, I've lived in that building the entire time I've been in New York. I've come to love it in both that building and that neighborhood, and it hurts to think of my home being wiped off the map. Not to mention I'm at an awkward middle ground with this. I have too much money to qualify for that affordable lottery, but not enough to buy a place in that new building... Where does that leave me?"

The developer let them talk before speaking again. "That's why we offered the buyout, to help you with moving to a new place. You've been in the building for a long time, the landlord says you've been a good tenant, so we made what we hoped was a generous offer."

"Only it's not enough to work with," they said, striving to keep their tone polite and firm at the same time.

The man's furrowed brow loosened a bit. "Are you saying that if you had enough to move, you'd leave the building and help us move forward with this?"

"That would make it possible, yes."

"Excuse me a moment." He rose and disappeared into another room. They glanced around the room and out the window. The afternoon sun sparkled on the Hudson River, but this stunning sight wasn't enough to distract them. They wished they had Justin to wrap his arms around them, Lena to step up for them, or even their mom to back them up in her own misguided but well-intentioned way. But they had to face this alone.

The developer returned to the room with a folder of paperwork. "I've explained your situation and looked into our budget for this project, and we are prepared to make another buyout offer. But this is the final one we can make. If you can't accept it, we'll have to take more drastic measures to keep this project on track."

He opened the folder and indicated the top page. Their eyes popped at the number, but they carefully schooled their face as their mind raced. This was much closer to what Barb had indicated they'd need … they had enough money saved to fill in the difference…

"That should be all right," they said evenly, as if they weren't negotiating their entire future.

"Good." The developer was equally nonchalant as he handed them a pen. "Then I'll need you to sign here … and here … turn the page … there…"

Charlie left the building with writer's cramp and a happier sense of shock than they were used to. In the span of a few minutes, their worst fears were wiped away. They could find a place that let them keep Willow, fit all their stuff, get taken a little more seriously as a buyer than as a renter… They walked to their bank branch in a daze, but their hand remained firmly clenched on their bag with the check that would help them find a new home.

Once the deposit was complete, they reached for their phone and touched a contact. They realized who they were calling as the phone rang, but didn't hang up. It felt too right, and they weren't stopping now.

****

Justin stuffed the last of his dirty clothes in the laundry bag, sealed it up, and folded it into the side of his suitcase as he planned the route in his head. The subway would spit him out right in Penn Station, a train would take him to New Jersey, and his parents would be waiting for him at the station. There was no reason to hang around New York anymore. Not to mention Janelle was way too polite to say she'd like to have her apartment to herself again, but she'd probably appreciate it.

His phone rang, and he immediately picked up at the sight of the caller. "Charlie?"

"Hi." The tone of their voice was hard to gauge, and traffic in the background didn't help.

"What's going on? Are you okay?"

"I had a meeting with the developer of the new building this morning, and he had some pretty interesting things to say."

He carefully measured his tone. "What happened?"

"Well, first I had to sit through a bit of a lecture on the importance of the project. But then, and this is the part I still can't believe, they asked me about my situation and actually listened to it. And offered to help with it."

He waited for them to continue. "What does that…"

"It means they upped the buyout enough that I can make a down payment someplace. It means I can buy something I'd actually want to live in and not settle."

Their words came out in a burst of joy, and a smile spread across his face. "Charlie, that's great."

"I've got to go. Of course I have to call my broker, but I also have to tell Lena. And Mom."

"You didn't yet?" he asked.

"No. I wanted you to be the first to know." They sounded as surprised as he felt.

"I'm glad I was." His racing heart spread warmth through his chest, and he asked, "Can I see you?"

"I'm on my way to Helga's now, but if you want to come to the courtyard…"

"I'll meet you there." There'd be other trains later, and he didn't want to miss this. He abandoned his packing and hailed a taxi.

Ashley smiled as he arrived at Helga's. "Hey, stranger. I haven't seen you in a while."

"I know." He paused. "Is Charlie here?"

"They're in the back." She gestured her head in that direction. Sure enough, they were sitting at a table with Janelle and a tall woman with dark, purple-streaked hair. He was too far away to hear the conversation, but their animated expression and gestures suggested they were telling the story of the meeting. It reminded him of similar conversations they'd had with him.

He had no trouble hearing the cheers that suggested they'd gotten to the end of the story, though. Both women hugged them, and he wished he could do the same. Janelle was facing the entrance and saw him, nodded to him, and nudged them.

Charlie's gaze landed on him, and they left the group. They didn't approach him all the way, but the look in their eyes was similar to the one they wore when they were about to launch themself into his arms. "Hey."

"Hey." Their expression looked happier than he'd seen it in weeks, but still unreadable. He schooled his own features against bursting out into a huge, stupid grin at the sight of them.

He smiled easily. "First off, congratulations. I'm glad it worked out for you."

"Thanks. Come on." They led him to the courtyard. That was where they'd decided to give him another chance every time something had gone wrong, a memory that wasn't lost on him as they looked around for a free table.

"So, what else is going on?" he asked once they were sitting across from him.

"That's what I'm trying to figure out. I know we said this was just for the summer even before the whole … thing, and I know we said our good-byes a few days ago. But I also know that when I found out, like I said, I wanted you to be the first to know. I want you to be the first to know everything that happens to me. Good, bad, ridiculous, serious…" Their voice trailed off as they gazed at him. "I know it's crazy."

"It's not. It makes more sense than you think

because you're the first person I think of with everything. Even when we weren't talking, I kept thinking, 'What would Charlie say about this?' and wishing I could see you."

"I wanted to see you, too, but I couldn't—can't— like we did before."

"What do you mean?"

"I still don't know how long you knew you were working there, and it doesn't matter now," they said before he could interrupt. "What does matter is that if we do decide to see each other, we both handle things better. I'll hear you out and not jump to conclusions, but you can't keep secrets from me."

The idea that there was still a chance opened Justin's heart a little wider with every word, and then it opened his mouth. "You want to hear my secrets? I told you nothing changed, and it still hasn't. Makes me doubt it ever will, seeing as I fell in love with you."

Their eyes widened, and they stayed quiet for so long that he wondered if he said too much. So what if he had? Charlie was the one who'd just insisted on no more secrets. And if he really didn't have anything to lose, there was no harm in laying everything out on the table.

Finally, their lips stretched into the smile he could never resist. "Nothing's changed for me, either. I don't know what's going to happen between us with school for you and the apartment hunt for me, but I do know it's worth trying to find out because I want more time with you. I've never met anyone as amazing, brave, or passionate as you, and I fell in love with you, too."

Through the whole conversation, both of them had been inching the chairs closer to each other. And at the last sentence, Charlie leaned forward. He pulled them onto his lap facing him, they wrapped their arms around his shoulders, and their kiss filled him with the most unexpected and wonderful feeling of completion. His cock reacted to having their groin against his again, but he didn't feel the need to rush into the restaurant's bathroom with them. Time and possibilities suddenly stretched ahead of him, and he welcomed the feeling.

"So what now?" they asked between kisses.

"Now … remember when you carded me at the beginning of the summer?"

"Yeah. You and Janelle both said you'd be twenty-eight in … August." Comprehension dawned on them, and they reached into his back pocket. "Let me see that ID again."

They squeezed his ass as they pulled out his wallet, and their eyes widened as they looked at the whole birth date on his driver's license. "Shit. Happy birthday! All I was looking at was the year … and then I completely … I don't even have a card, but we can still…"

He touched his lips to theirs to silence them. "You have you." As he pulled them close and the kiss deepened, he couldn't imagine what they would have bought that he'd possibly want more than this.

Epilogue

December 2013

Charlie opened their eyes to find Willow staring straight at them. They'd dismantled the bed with some help from Justin last night, and the two of them had slept on the mattress on the floor. As much as they liked waking up by his side, it wasn't enough to cancel out the weirdness of waking up at eye level with their cat.

They gently slid out so as not to wake him, got up, and poured a small baggie of dry cat food on a paper towel. After she finished breakfast, they gave her a treat filled with a sedative the vet had recommended. A small twinge of guilt stabbed at them as she stood on her hind legs and daintily took it from their hand, but it was the only way they could be sure she wouldn't panic on the ride to the new apartment.

A short time later, as Charlie packed up the sheets and the clothes they'd slept in, Justin stacked the bare mattress against the wall. "Could that be everything?" he asked, stepping back.

They glanced around a suddenly spacious apartment. "It looks like it."

"Then I'd better get ready for my interview. Janelle said I could shower and change at her place."

"Go for it. And thank her for keeping Helga's open today. That's the most help she could give me and Lena."

He didn't leave right away. "I wish this was any day but today. I tried to reschedule, but otherwise she couldn't have seen me until it was too late to register for spring."

"And how much have you helped me pack in the past few weeks? This is more important than lugging a few boxes."

"I'll come over with dinner tonight and help you set up the place."

"You were going to come over tonight anyway."

"True. Tell Ryan I said hi."

Charlie grinned. "Will do." Over the past few months, Ryan and Justin would often be the last two waiting at the bar while they closed up with Lena. The two guys had gone from warily eyeing each other to making small talk to forming the beginnings of a friendship.

They pulled him close. "*Merde*. I love you."

Justin smiled at their words and returned their embrace. "I love you, too."

Nearly four months later, the sound of the words on their ears and feel on their lips still hadn't gotten old. He headed uptown, and they took one more look around a room empty but for the small mountain of boxes and disassembled furniture. One way or another, their time here was up. They'd alternated between tears of grief and giddy excitement at the impending move. Now that it was here, all they felt was peace, acceptance, and readiness for what lay ahead.

A few hours later, Lena looked at the address on the phone propped to the van's dashboard. "Charlie, do you think you're *ever* going to move west of Second Avenue?"

"Now why would I do that?" Their tone was joking, but their answer was a serious one. Even with the extra boost from the buyout, Murray Hill and Yorkville had been some of the only Manhattan neighborhoods they could even consider buying in. Their new apartment was on Eighty-eighth Street between First and York Avenues, which wasn't unmanageably far from Helga's and would give them gorgeous views of the East River from their new bedroom.

"Better transportation, for one thing," Ryan said from behind the wheel. As the most recent New York transplant, he was also the one still most used to driving. He'd commandeered the van from his family's upstate farm to help with the boxes from Charlie's apartment. The U-Haul behind it was filled with their small stock of furniture and helmed by Kelsey and some of the guys on her team.

"It's nothing I'm not used to. And hey, we can't all live happily ever after on the Hudson."

Lena turned, probably to roll her eyes at them, but her eyes swept over Ryan on the way and softened. His eyes flicked towards her, and his face melted into a smile. His hands were still on the wheel and her hands were in her lap, but the connection between the two of them was as palpable as if he'd taken her in his arms.

Charlie would have been sickened by their friend's behavior if they didn't know exactly how she felt. A few months had passed since they'd gotten back together with Justin, and that wasn't enough time for their feelings for him to fade. The memory of his internship had faded into the background along with the other early missteps with him.

The present and future were more important than the past. And in the present, the two of them talked every night and saw each other as often as two busy schedules would allow. And if things went the way they hoped, they'd be seeing a lot more of him and able to think about what was next for the two of them.

At a red light, Lena reached into the box on her lap. She took a bite of a chocolate doughnut with crushed candy canes embedded in white frosting and closed her eyes in ecstasy. "Okay, I get that we don't have bakeries like this near me, but…"

"But I got the business card like you asked me to,

and I can always have a doughnut and coffee as usual once they sign the contract." The bakery's planned partnership with Helga's wasn't the only way Charlie could bring a bit of the Lower East Side to Yorkville with them. Sawasdee Amigos' second branch would open a few blocks from their new place in March.

As Ryan drove to the new building, Charlie slipped their free hand into the cat carrier to pet a drowsy Willow as they thought about what lay ahead. They knew they could always take the subway downtown if they got too homesick, but would they need to do that with all the places to explore and try around their new place? Charlie wasn't just looking for a new place to keep their stuff; they were looking for a new place to live, and this new neighborhood had checked out.

Hours later, it was already dark, and the small, bright apartment was filled with boxes of Charlie's stuff. "I really appreciate everything," they said, handing out laminated cards. "I can take care of the rest, but only because you've done so much. I'll be back at work next week once I've settled everything here. Come see me then, and don't forget these."

One of the firefighters smiled as he glanced at the free drink card. "Sweet. Can't wait to see what Beethoven at the bar will come up with next."

Charlie tried not to sigh too loud or roll their eyes—after all, the guy had just given up his day off to help them move. The *New York Scene* writer had bestowed the nickname on them in the story he'd written after a conversation that had touched on their sobriety, which they'd held onto even in the stress of the search and move, and all they could do was wonder how they of all people had been given a name shared with an oversized animal yet again.

At the same time, the stupid sobriquet was the

only bad thing to come out of that article. Their nonalcoholic cocktails had proven a surprising draw, and Lena had been over the moon when a clique of models had come in for those drinks on Fashion Week. It had led to great press, including a hit on Page Six, and the compliments from a Victoria's Secret angel had been good for their ego, too.

After Charlie thanked everyone again and hugged Kelsey, Lena, and Ryan, they let Willow out of her carrier. She was coming out of the sedative and eager to explore, so they left her to it as they started to put their new home together. They thoughtfully glanced around the room and the mountain of boxes, trying to imagine how it would look once this mess was cleared out. And the sooner the better—they'd seen a guy selling Christmas trees a few blocks from here, and one would look good in that corner by the window. Not to mention it would be especially easy now that their ornaments were right here instead in basement storage.

Charlie shook their head and reminded themself not to get too far ahead of things—there was no sense setting up a Christmas tree when they didn't even have their rooms unpacked yet. They pulled on their dark green parka and headed out for a quick bodega run.

Back home—it would take some time to think of the new place that way—they put the bag of staples in the kitchen, opened the duffel bag with the items they'd need the soonest, and pulled out a towel, bar of soap, and their favorite Malin + Goetz shampoo. They hadn't gotten to shower this morning and desperately needed one now.

About fifteen minutes later, they returned to the stack of boxes with renewed vigor from the warmth and water pressure of the new shower. The first thing they saw was a package from their parents with a note reading

Do not open until moved in scribbled on the wrappings. They opened it to find a set of high-thread-count sheets and a plush blanket. The card read, *Dear Charlie, We hope these give you a good night's sleep in your new place. Love, Mom and Dad.*

The properly addressed message warmed their heart as much as the gift inside, and they used it to make the bed set up in their new room. Thirty-two was too old to spend another night sleeping practically on the floor, and there were other things they didn't want to do there, either. The stress of the move and the college interview had been real mood killers over the past few days, but they were getting into it again.

As if they'd conjured him, a melodic chime, as opposed to their old buzzer, went off to interrupt their delicious imaginings. The man outside looked weirdly distorted on camera, but there was no mistaking Justin. They studied the panel for a moment before finding the button that would welcome him up. As he climbed the stairs, their excitement mounted for what lay ahead, both with him and in all aspects of life in their new home.

****

The dean looked over the transcript and resume on her desk. "Well, Justin, you have one of the more interesting backgrounds I've ever seen—a ballet career before college, good grades, and then an internship with Bernardo Herrera. Can you tell me more about that work experience?"

Justin took a breath to gather his thoughts. "I'm glad I did it. It gave me a lot to think about. It made me see that while I'm interested in architecture, I don't want to be a part of something that's going to be a huge aberration on the area it's going up in. When I told my advisor about that, she told me to consider adding some urban planning classes to my curriculum. And admitted that the school didn't have enough, which is how I find myself here today."

The dean nodded, but seemed more interested in another topic. "What was Bernardo Herrera like?"

Justin bit back a smile. "I didn't spend much time with him." He spoke diplomatically now, but hadn't been able to hide his glee when he'd found out his old boss had been fired from the Lower East Side project for making too many demands that turned out to be unmanageable. The event had resulted in tantrums from the architect and more time for Charlie and others in the building to find new homes. He couldn't decide what thought made him happier—the idea of something less ridiculous going up on the site or the news through social media that Denise had quit and gone to another firm, where she was playing an active role on a team designing an affordable housing complex for formerly homeless New Yorkers with AIDS.

"Maybe that's for the best, if the rumors about his ego are true." The middle-aged woman gave him a real smile. "Well, Justin, I think that's about everything we need for now. Did you have any questions?"

"I don't think so, only because everything makes so much sense," he said. "And I have your email if any come up."

"Then we'll keep an eye out for your most recent records so we can further advise in your course of study. We look forward to welcoming you in the spring semester."

Justin shook her hand and left the campus with an excitement that he hadn't even experienced when he'd gotten the internship. It was underscored by a sense of purpose he hadn't felt since he'd taken the apprenticeship that had turned into a career with the Boston Ballet. He'd gone back to New Jersey and taken his first full-time round of architecture classes in the fall semester, but knew he was doing the right thing by transferring to Hunter College to do a double major.

None of it had been as easy as it sounded. While Janelle had encouraged the ideas of him choosing a better fitting major and being able to see him more often, his parents hadn't exactly been receptive to him changing colleges and his course of study yet again. As a matter of fact, his dad was meeting him and Janelle at Helga's to discuss it.

"How'd it go?" Stanley asked after a few bites of the shared potato pizza appetizer.

"Great," Justin said. "It's a good campus, and everyone I met was really nice and helpful. It looks like I can apply some of the classes I already took to this program, but there's still a lot to learn. I have a good feeling about this."

His dad frowned. "As I recall, you said the same thing when you decided to switch from pre-med to an English major. So you'll excuse me if I ask how you can be sure of that this time. You can't keep changing colleges and majors the way other people change their underwear."

"Dad!" Janelle protested.

Justin appreciated his sister's support, but stood his ground. "I get how you'd think that after those first few false starts, but this isn't one. The internship honed my focus, forced me to think about what I want and don't want, and it showed me that my current school won't let me move in that direction. Doubling like this gives me so many more options than the others did, and it's better for me here. There's more to help me stay focused. I won't be confined to a college campus where there's nothing to do but drink and party. Janelle's around, and I have my love to keep me on track."

"Mm-hmm." His dad hadn't met Charlie yet, and his brow furrowed in confusion. "I keep meaning to ask … are you seeing a man or a woman, anyway? I saw the pictures you posted, and you both look happy, but I just can't figure out…"

Justin smiled before his sister could answer. "Charlie defies all categories, and I wouldn't want them any other way."

Stanley seemingly gave up on him and turned to Janelle. "What does he mean by that?"

Before she could answer, a waiter approached the table. "Your order to go is ready."

"Thanks. I'll see you, all of you, later." He took the bag, hugged his pleased sister and confused father good-bye, and stepped out into the chilly night. Another great advantage of Hunter was that it was just a few subway stops from both Helga's and Charlie's new place. He descended the stairs, reminded himself to head for the uptown local track from now on, and couldn't keep the smile off his face as he got on the incoming train.

It would have been more fun to give them a Christmas card with his acceptance letter inside, but their insistence on no more secrets had closed the door on that idea. At the same time, it had opened both their lives to each other. They'd looked over the course descriptions with him and brought him along to open houses of the places they'd liked best. Charlie had chosen their current place on their own, but had kept reminding him how much they wanted his input.

The memory of everything that had happened in the recent past reminded him of his hopes for the future. He'd move into the dorms in a few weeks, but there was no reason he had to spend every night there. He and Charlie could spend his last semesters of college working things out, getting to know each other even better, and taking advantage of the luxury of time to let their love grow. Maybe things would even reach a point where he could move in with them after graduation.

He headed up two flights, already an improvement on the old place. They'd opened the door for him, and stood grinning against a backdrop of boxes. He kissed them hello, then bent to scratch Willow's ears. She nuzzled his hand before resuming her dive in and out of an empty box. Something suggested she could keep it up all night.

"Looks good," he said, taking off his coat and glancing around. He'd visited the apartment with Charlie when they'd narrowed down their choices, and was still so proud of them for taking the plunge with it.

"You're being nice. There's still so much to do."

"And it still looks like you already."

They ushered him in. The room was nowhere near unpacked, but their couch was already set up against a wall facing the decorative fireplace. "How'd it go today?" they asked.

He grinned. "I'm officially in."

"Great!" Their smile widened to match his. "I picked up some glasses while I was out, and I'd already gotten something special for tonight. I'm glad it's special for both of us."

They reached in the fridge and opened a chilling bottle. The label said it was nonalcoholic, but the sparkle and pop of the cork matched that of any champagne he'd ever had. Once both plastic glasses were poured, Charlie raised theirs. "Cheers."

"To what?" he asked.

They thought it over before smiling. "To new beginnings, and to being with you for whatever lies ahead."

He smiled. "I'll drink to that."

They touched their glass to his and took a sip. He followed their lead and smiled at the taste of the sparkling drink. It was cold, crisp, and not overly sweet. "Very nice. How will it pair with this?" he asked, holding up the bag.

"Whatever it is, beautifully. Thanks for getting it."

He brought the containers to the table, and the rest of the meal passed with excited talk about plans for the apartment, the new semester, and the upcoming holidays.

After both glasses and the dinner containers were empty, Charlie stood. "Want to see the rest of it?"

"Sure." It had been a while since the open house, and the place would look completely different with their possessions and mark on it.

They led him down the short hall, pointing out the updated galley kitchen, full bath, and small closet where they'd install a washer/dryer as soon as time and finances would allow. At the end of the hall, the sight of the familiar bed in a new room got his attention. "I see you got this set up already."

They stepped a little closer. "Well, I had to."

All the meanings of their statement drove home how close they were standing to him, and he pulled them to his chest to close the last inches of distance. They wrapped their arms around him and leaned up to bring their lips to his. He'd been concerned that they might be too tired for this, but the ardor of their kisses and the way they pressed into him suggested otherwise.

They pulled their sweater over their head as they backed towards the bed, and Justin undid the buttons on his dress shirt. Once both sets of clothes were gone, a process interrupted by several kisses and strokes, they lay down on the bed. He leaned over them and teased his bare, hard cock against Charlie before plunging in.

A gratified moan escaped Charlie as he entered, and they moved their hips along with his thrusts. All the while, he appreciated the freedom and intimacy anew. He had taken advantage of his school's health center shortly after returning to campus, and they'd gone for a checkup of their own around the same time. After both sets of tests had come back negative, he'd dumped the last of his condoms into the bowl of freebies at the health center. Now they moaned as they clenched tighter around him, and his own unfettered climax followed.

As he pulled out, he looked over to see a smile on their face. "First time for everything," they said before drifting off to sleep.

Justin looked fondly at them. He liked to think that he somehow would have met them no matter what. And yet, if his injury and that ridiculous internship had happened to send him to the love of his life, it was amazing how good things could come out of bad. *They* were amazing, and he fell asleep dreaming of all the firsts that still lay ahead with them.

The End

ACKNOWLEDGEMENTS

Charlie's experiences as a gender-fluid person should be read as those of an individual, not universally. My thanks to Svetla Rose for helping me tell their story with the utmost accuracy and sensitivity.

Additionally, Charlie's experiences in the New York real estate world should not be read as typical. I've taken some creative liberties, but thank Ondel Hylton for the advice and insights that keep their happy ending grounded in reality.

AN ESPECIALLY HOT SUMMER

EVERNIGHT PUBLISHING ®

www.evernightpublishing.com

www.ingramcontent.com/pod-product-compliance
Lightning Source LLC
Chambersburg PA
CBHW050043180626
46810CB00002B/861